TURN TO THE RIVER

L.P. Ballard

www.turntotheriver.com

@turn.to.the.river

Dedicated to my Grandparents
Iris & Peter Day and Thelma & Ron Ballard

London is, and always has been divided.
Wealth, politics, culture; the city is fractured.
Fragments of society move at different speeds.
It's at the cracks and edges where friction is
greatest.

PART I

1   ANTI

Day or night? Decembers in London give nothing away. Gloom ridden, the darkness barely yielding to the overcast dawn. It was still early, Grayson Day knew that much as he stirred awake for the second time that morning. Far too early. Still exhausted.

Conscious jolted. He was not alone.

He gathered vision from the haze.

At the foot of the bed towered a jet black silhouette.

The figure stood motionless.

A shrouded hood framed an enraged stare, fixed on Grayson, it did not yield. Dark skin glistened as perspiration beaded from his forehead and ran down to his sharp stubbled jawline.

Broad shoulders steamed as they rose and released with

each breath.

His eyes widened as he acknowledged recognition.

Tutting, his head motioned side-to-side. The tuts descended in tone, each more pronounced than the last as he snapped his tongue harder from his teeth.

His torso flexed, defined biceps pulsed and drew Grayson's attention down towards his clenched fists, bound tight with black tape.

With intent, he raised his left and released the grip.

His stare on Grayson did not break.

As he swung his right fist and struck it deep into the exposed left palm, a thunderous slap rang round the room.

If he hadn't already, he now had Grayson's full attention.

Any remnants from a heavy head were pushed aside as adrenaline coursed.

He shuddered as he stared up at the figure of Joel Olakunbi.

Wrong or right? Grayson, now wired, tried to comprehend how he could have been exposed so quickly. It had only been a matter of hours since, for the first time in his life, he had betrayed his best friend.

Black or white? It wasn't that simple. He made the decision for Joel's own good, but how was he to know. Now seeing the venom in his friend's eyes, Grayson began to question that decision.

Fight or flight? The stillness snapped. Joel surged towards him and in one stride he mounted the bed.

Grayson drove his legs downwards and pushed his back up into the wall.

It gave him a beat, a second to evade an oncoming shot, but it was not enough.

Joel's fist swung in, Grayson couldn't raise his guard in time. An open palm struck him across the face. The course tape stung as it ripped his cheek.

Sitting prone, he threw an arm up in defence. A swipe rode the block and clipped the top of his head. Again an open palm shot.

'Look at you bruv.' Joel said.

Grayson's vision impaired by flashes of sharp deliberate movement.

'You're a fucking mess.'

He held his elbows high to protect his head as the blows rocked him left and right.

'Come on! Is that all you've got?'

Finding himself in a headlock, his face buried into Joel's midriff. He gasped for air and thrashed in a vain attempt to escape the vice like hold.

His energy was quick to deplete. He was trapped.

As knuckles went to work on his scalp, Grayson resigned to his fate, but it occurred to him that the initial strikes had not hurt him at all. In fact, he wasn't in pain, just shock.

His heart continued to race, but a realisation set in. And with that realisation, relief.

This wasn't revenge. There was no malice in the aggression. This was just Joel being Joel, large in stature and naive to his power and far too full of energy. Yes, that was Joel.

Most would find it agressive, over the top, but for them a hard punch or two, or a bit of roughhousing as a greeting was an ordinary part of their inseparable twenty-two-year friendship.

Far too exhausted to form any sort of counter Grayson collapsed.

'Fuck. Seriously!' He said, as he tried to catch his breath, 'I'm in fucking pieces here.'

Joel released his grip and rocked backward on the bed in hysterics.

'Thought you should get involved in some training.'

'For the love of God. It's Saturday morning. Give it a rest.'

He tried to remain stern, but his grin betrayed him.

'You're such a prick.'

'Come on. No time for rest. I thought we agreed? It's all business now.' Joel said as he jumped up from the bed into a skip.

'Ten kilos to go, four weeks until weigh-in. Thought I would run over here and get your lazy arse outta bed. I need a training partner and you need to stop moping around coz Estella dumped you.' He threw some air punches to maintain his sweat and continued, 'It's probably a good thing bruv. Now's not the time for distractions.'

Grayson rolled his eyes at the insinuation.

'Don't be a dick. You're half the reason she ended it.'

'We both know that's not true bruv. Still, fact is you need to get over her. She does this all the time. The moment we have some business to attend to, she causes drama.'

'It's not like that. She just wants what's best for me.'

'What? And what's best for you is keep messin' you up like this?'

'Look. I'm too tired for this shit right now.'

He turned his head to resign from the conversation and glanced across to the empty side of the bed. Relieved that Joel was yet to find out about the events of the night before and even more relieved he hadn't arrived an hour or so earlier.

'Look. You just do what you do best,' he nodded towards the strapping that bound Joel's hands, 'and leave Estella to me. Focus on the fight. You fucked up, whether you want to admit it or not. And the only way back is to win the fight and put things straight. You owe that to Ama and Kamsi. It is the least you could do for them, for looking after your broke ass all these years.'

'Yes bruv, stop goin' on about it yeah? They looked after you as well don't forget. Anyway, I've got it, yeah? That's why I'm here, putting in the work. Perhaps you should as well?' Joel said, as he continued to bound and throw jabs.

'Not today. I'm shattered. Anyway how did you get in here? You could have knocked, rather than scare the shit out of me.'

'Where's the fun in that? It'll teach you to leave your spare set of keys with a couple of old women and not me.' Joel jangled a set of door keys in front of Grayson's face.

'Old women. Ha. Don't let 'em hear you say that. They may be middle aged, but they'd box you about no end. Aunties privilege.'

Grayson recognised the keys as the spare set he had given Ama and Kamsi shortly after moving across London into his apartment in the West End.

Joel sized up the room.

'It may be fancy up these ends, but you really need to take more care fam. And sort out your security.' He flicked his head backwards and offered up one last tut.

'Anyways. Suit yourself. Later yeah?'

His broad smile cracked again with laughter as he bobbed and weaved behind a raised guard and backed his way to the door.

As Joel left, Grayson collapsed back to his pillow. Mind slow to function. Relieved Joel had not yet found out what he had done, but it would only be a matter of time before he did. If all went well, Grayson would have time to sit him down and explain things before he found out. Before things got out of hand.

He took a few deep breaths as he resisted engaging with the torrent of memories from the night before that now rushed towards him. His relief would be short lived. He knew that as soon as the fog lifted they would drown him. He had set off a chain of events that would warrant retribution. The clock was already ticking.

He started to run through his plan. Things had not gone the way he expected. He now had to adapt.

He was deep in concentration when his phone began to vibrate on the side table.

Who would call this early on a Saturday morning?

He swung his legs from the bed. Sat-up, but was still arched in exhaustion. He looked across the room to the full length mirror propped against the wall, waiting to be hung. He assessed the damage from the heavy nights drinking in his pale reflection. He clasped and stretched his jaw, ran his thumb across his freckled complexion and over the deep scar below his left eye.

Beyond the cursory few rings, the phone continued to vibrate.

As if a moments flicker would disturb him from his crucial train of thought, he reached across to the side table, but kept his eyes fixed on their deep blue reflection. What have you got yourself into?

His hand flailed on the side table. On the third attempt he located and clasped his phone and swung it in to his line of sight.

The caller ID read: Ama Olakunbi.

Grayson answered with a scattered voice.

He was met with the sound of agonised wailing.

'Ama. Ama. Ams. What's the matter? What is it?'

'It's, it's, it's Kamsi!' she wept.

'Ams, what about Kamsi? What's the matter?'

'She's. She's dead!'

2 TILT

♠ *10 Days Earlier* ♠

He shouldn't be there. Something all too familiar had led him to this point. He ought to resist. Physically, he was strong. This was a weakness of the mind. More specifically, self-control.

Sat in the low-lit room, the stitched leather chair too small for his frame. Off the estate, he was out of place. A laid-back posture alluded to the confidence he wished to show but did not feel. A calm smile suggested that he was in command, but at this moment, he was far from it.

He peered under the two cards face-down in front of him. The odds he knew by heart. For years he and his best friend

Grayson Day, had studied the game. They had taught themselves the best strategies for every scenario.

Through the lingering cigar smoke, he monitored the other players. To track the subtlest tells, he needed to concentrate, but he couldn't focus. Jaw clenched, pangs of guilt ached in his stomach. Distracting thoughts kept surfacing, trying to understand the forces that had lured him there.

It started as the greatest day of his life. Recognition of his breakthrough; celebrating with his loved ones, those that had fought hard to support him and to get him to this point. His first professional boxing sponsorship contract.

Come on, concentrate.

Why leave his celebration lunch? Did his aunties believe his excuse? Questions fought their way to the forefront of his mind, distracting him from the task at hand.

He looked again at his cards, five and seven, different suits. Terrible cards. As his turn comes, he slides them forward on the crimson felt.

'Fold,' he says, dismissively.

He needs to analyse and study the other players, but his conscience continues to bombard him. Why come here? Why play such high stakes? Another pang of guilt, his focus blurred by the mounting list of questions circling in his head. He can't block them; they corner him as he tries to fight back.

A couple more hands. He was down, but a good run, and he'll soon be up straight. Chasing-a-loss was a textbook strategy to fail. He had seen others in this position a hundred times before, but it was the first time for him at such high stakes. New to the gut-wrenching sickness of losing more than he could afford. The realisation he was failing those he loved.

As a finely tuned athlete, his stamina was first class. Even so, he was tired, exerting vast amounts of energy to mask frustration at the cards dealt to him. Nine and five, again different suits. More bad cards. Another hand to fold. Three hours of cold cards were taking its toll. He urged himself to concentrate, to get a read on this hand. Something to help him as he continued the fight.

In the ring, as at the poker table, he preferred an aggressive strategy, but he knew the game too well to play such terrible cards. However, he considered, perhaps if he used that aggressive strategy against his conscience it would help? As he adopted this thought, his questions of self-doubt took on an alternative form. Why shouldn't he be here? It's his money. He earned it! He can spend the money as he pleased! It was a weak attempt to shed the regret of the money he had lost so far that evening. Almost ten thousand pounds.

He tries hard to convince and overpower his conscience, but the resistance is strong and the retorts are cutting. Dry mouthed, he reaches for a glass and finds it empty. As a thought develops, he tries to resist it, but fighting it only brings it to life. He shudders as it reaches full form. Ama and Kamsi could have done so much with that money! His head dipped. As he pictures them, the shame overwhelms him. He was used to taking hard blows and fighting on, but not self-inflicted shots to the gut. This last shot winded him.

His hands, tools of his trade, usually so steady, were now shaking. Eyes glazed over. Thoughts of his aunties floored him in shame. At the point of resignation and throwing in the towel, he reached for the new cards dealt to him.

Ace (hearts) - Ace (diamonds).

The two bright red A's shone like a wink from the devil. At the sight, a shot of adrenaline broke him from the malaise. Finally. Good cards and with a good position on the table. The hand he had been waiting for.

Not too assertive, he tells himself. He had the tendency to

fight too hard, too early, but he had trained hard to breathe, take his time and damper his excitement as his heart rate quickened. To stay patient and pick his shot.

A small raise. It should at the least create value and if met with a call, that would be ideal.

'Raise to 400.' He said, just audible for the players at the table to hear.

The player to his left calls and matches the bet. A smooth-skinned Persian, small in stature, wearing a casual maroon sports jacket, high-end designer label. A statue-like demeanour, emotionless, sharp-featured face, part hidden by stylish sunglasses.

The next player, a suit-wearing city type, folds his cards.

Another call from the player whom he knew only as Mr Shevchuk, having overheard the concierge address him earlier. Heavyset in a checked blue shirt, navy jacket and a gold chain. Thinning grey hair, pushed back from a permanent frown etched into his forehead. Bloated, Shevchuk continually fidgeted in his chair.

Two more folds to his right, in quick succession.

His guilt subsided too easily. Now three players in the hand. He salivates at the situation. He has the strongest cards possible, and the pot is already over twelve hundred pounds.

Out comes the flop. The dealer places three community cards in the middle of the table.

Ace (clubs) - Queen (spades) - 5 (diamonds).

Another surge of adrenaline washes away any remaining shreds of remorse. He now has three Aces, top-set. He still had the strongest hand possible.

'Check.' From Shevchuk, as he taps the table.

He was alert, focused. Time to make the money back.

Time for a set-up jab.

'Raise 800.' He said, in a deep, confident voice. The declaration made in a distinctive East End tone rounded off by the hint of a Nigerian accent.

As he pushed a stack of chips forward in his peripheral vision, he noticed the Persian glance down to his chips. The tell was very subtle. Most would not see it, but for him the read was clear. For years he had been studying reactions: a hand movement here, a glance there, even the dilation of his opponent's pupils. Knowing when to strike. That was his livelihood. If you could call it that.

He had the Persian on trip-queens, three queens. He was sure of it. Two in his hand and one on the table. He expected the call from him. Three queens; the second best hand out there. Second only to his. He had him trapped.

The pangs of guilt gone. His abdominal muscles were still tight, guilt now replaced by rushes of excitement. Emotions he had to contain and disguise from the others at the table.

Shevchuk's call came as a surprise.

His head jolted upwards. He hadn't even tried to garner a read. Shevchuk could not have strong cards. And with two players committed to the pot, he should have folded.

Puzzled, but with a wry confident smile, he ran through the possibilities and calculated the odds. A method that any reasonable player would undertake. The best did so instantaneously, perhaps without the grin.

Having run through all the scenarios possible, he concluded that a player such as Shevchuk should not have invested twelve hundred pounds into this hand. Perhaps he was tiring? Was the old man's guard dropping?

The dealer laid the turn card on to the table, the fourth community card.

Ace (spades).

A rush of excitement passed through him as he looked down. The perfect card. He now had four Aces. He tried hard to contain himself. Thoughts of his celebration lunch, the excuses he made, and his aunties disappointment had vanished. He was back in control. The comeback music began to play in his head.

He expected the 'check' that followed from Shevchuk. Through a cloud of cigar smoke hanging under the light fitting, he studied the man as he again repositioned in the chair. Maybe, just maybe, he made his full-house and was playing coy. With four Aces he would certainly indulge 'Mr' Shevchuk.

Convinced that any further action would see a fold from the Persian, he could play strong now, by either buying the pot or being called. Either way, he'd win.

Or he could let the river card, the fifth community card, come out. Perhaps the Persian would pick up a fourth Queen. The ultimate trap, for maximum payout. The comeback music was now reaching a crescendo. He had to resist humming along and throwing air punches.

He decided on the latter strategy. A 'check' from the Persian followed his 'check'. And the dealer dealt the river card.

Jack (spades).

He didn't want to see a 10, Jack or King of spades. They were the only cards that could cause him a problem. He shrugged off the thought, Shevchuk was sitting on his full-house. He was certain of it. Only confirmed when the heavyset man leaned forward and grunted as he pushed his chips forward with a mid-position raise.

'Raise 1,600.' Shevchuk announced, locking eyes with his opponent. His hand retracted from the chips with purpose, his shirt cuff now exposed from the jacket sleeve. With it a heavy gold watch, loose on his wrist.

Perfect. With that bet, Shevchuk was looking for value. He peered down at his chips a stack of 6,600 that remained from the original 15,000 he bought in with four hours earlier.

This pot would bring him back into profit. His options were to cash out, go home with a draw. Or fight on with confidence into the later rounds, like a true champion, a comeback from the death. Down, but never out.

'All-In!' he announced.

The fold from the Persian to his left was inevitable. He now focused on Shevchuk. The trap landed. Relishing the moment, he waited for Shevchuk to fold, or turn over his Five-Five.

Such a large pot assured amateur dramatics. It was the largest pot of the night by far.

Shevchuk took a deep breath, his frown sunk further into his forehead as he stared down and double checked his cards. He placed his left hand on his chest, and with his thumb stroked the cross hanging from the centre of his gold chain. In what sounded like a Ukrainian accent, low and unsettling, he murmured.

'Put on the full armour of God, so you can take your stand against the devil's schemes.'

On making this somewhat odd but chilling declaration, his frown released the grip on his forehead as he looked up and again locked eyes. He turned his cards, flipping them on to the centre of the table.

King (spades), 10 (spades).

Royal Flush.

It took time to process.

He tried to comprehend. His thoughts became layered,

grating, and shredding. His aunties. Everything they had done for him. Saved his life, raised him boy-to-man. What kind of a man was he? Wasting money they would work a year to earn.

The air in the room grew thick, breathing difficult. The previously mellow cigar smoke now repugnant.

He stood from his seat, focus blurred, the walls spun. Balance faltering, he backed heavy footed, weak-kneed, away from the table, staring in disbelief at what had happened.

He collapsed into a sofa in the main ballroom, head in hands. The lights dazed, laughter from the other tables screeched. The shame flooded back, an aching guilt he had never experienced. His chest was tight, breaths more like gasps. What had become of the day?

Ten minutes passed. Motionless, lost in regret. Broken pride. Shattered in remorse. He had made a small, but fatal mistake.

He stood, legs still unsure, head hung in defeat. He stumbled to the door. He had taken bad beats, but not like this. Taken down, from the turn to the river. Knocked-out by one card. A two-percent chance. Ninety-eight times from a hundred he would win that hand.

The concierge opened the door as he staggered across the foyer. A chilling wet winter breeze blew in. He had played it by-the-book, exactly how he was supposed to.

Unlucky? Unfair? Unjust? He didn't know which. His entire life he had fought the odds, fought against the system.

A grimace crossed his face. Determined, he turned.

No resistance. No control.

He paced back towards the cashier's desk, opened his wallet, and slid his card across the counter.

'Another fifteen thousand.'

3 FAMILY POT

CROWN & SCEPTRE, GREAT TITCHFIELD STREET, FITZROVIA, W1

30 NOVEMBER 2017

Sleet fell, faces grimaced. Rushed late-evening commuters did not look up. They did not notice or care for the festive lights that lined Regent Street. Soaked, they filed along the busy street into Oxford Circus tube station as directly as possible, before the coldness seeped through their jackets into their bones. Shoulders clattered hard against Grayson Day as he passed. If they wanted to walk with their heads down and pay no attention, it wasn't his responsibility to move out of their way. He was not in a conciliatory mood. His expression would have shown that, had it been possible to see beneath his black hooded coat. Hands high in his pockets, his posture braced for the contact.

For those that stayed in town after work, Christmas drinking season was well underway; punters escaping the dark wet evenings. Amber lighting and festive hospitality drawing them in like moths-to-a-flame to every pub across London's West End. The *Crown and Sceptre*, on Great Titchfield Street, was no different, bursting at the seams. Chatter and so-called atmosphere. Fine, orange-cinnamon sweetness now eclipsed the dank beer smell. And yes, what did he expect? Thursday evenings always the busiest, no matter the time of year. Next-day hangovers more manageable on company time. But having to squeeze through a bunch of obnoxious suit-wearing-wankers, using festive drinks as an excuse to feel up their receptionist, it just didn't seem worth it.

He didn't feel right. He wasn't himself. A restless peripheral tension had him on edge. It frustrated him, he couldn't determine the source. As he paced up the street, he pulled his phone from his pocket to check the time. He was over thirty minutes late.

He wanted to see Estella, but was reluctant. He knew the significance of where she had asked him to meet. The same pub where, four years earlier, they had toasted Grayson's move to the West End. The start of something new. Away from the distractions.

She was sentimental like that. Places, events, moments. They were important to her, but tonight Grayson had resigned to the fact the location was selected to send him a message and he already knew what that message would be. Her patience had run its course. It was the same old issue. The same thing that had kept their relationship so on'n'off for as long as they had known each other. Whilst she was the only girl that had ever tried to understand him, even she had grown tired of the distance he maintained, the fact that he wouldn't let her close. He closed-up and kept her on the outside. She had told him this countless times and even though they would always reconcile, she had promised him that this time would be the last.

As he arrived at the pub, he peered through a small unmisted section of the window. Sat towards the back, Estella stood out in the crowd. Beautiful. Shoulder length crazy blond curls, delicate skin and large innocent eyes, her slender figure perched on a high stool. In front of her an empty wine glass sat on a high table.

He squeezed his way through the door and maintained sight of her over the crowd as he edged around the bar. As she noticed him her expression brightened before falling solemn.

'Baltic out there.' He said, as he arrived at the table, now reading her expression up close. He reached out for a kiss. As he leaned in her head turned to cheek.

'Another drink?' He gestured to the empty glass on the table, as he placed his jacket on a vacant stool.

'No, thank you.' She said, as he sat.

'Look. It's great news about the sponsorship and I'm sorry I couldn't make the lunch to celebrate with all of you. It wouldn't have been right. You know, the way things have been. I hope you had a nice time.'

'It was fine.' Grayson responded with a shrug. 'What do you mean, the way things have been?' He knew the answer and in any case, wasn't particularly good at playing dumb.

She reached across and placed a delicate hand on his cheek. Her thumb caressed his angular cheekbone, then the scar below his eye, as her fingers ran through his disheveled brown hair.

'We can't go on like this.'

Here it comes, he thought.

'You know how much I care for you,' the intensity of her blue eyes mellowed as they sought his understanding, 'I always have, but it's not enough. Nothing has changed. I can't waste my life waiting for you to realise that.'

She searched for a response. There was none.

'This is what I mean. You don't talk to me Grayson. You're always so distant.'

She stood to leave.

'I'm sorry, but I can't do this anymore.'

He wanted to stop her, tell her he would change. That she was the most important thing in his life, but instead his shoulders sank as she turned and made her way to the door and left.

He sat in stoney silence, his eyes fixed to the stool she had vacated. He had known at some point she would leave him. Everyone he loved would leave eventually. They always did.

He went to order a drink. He dropped his shoulder into a gap and pushed through to the bar. A half-cut guy shunned by the movement and reared-up, but as soon as he made eye contact with Grayson, detected his mood and a glint of aggression he backed off. Grayson proceeded to order two double measures of whisky. The first he drank in one go, the second he raised slowly to his lips as he observed the drunken merriment as a Bing Crosby Christmas classic rang out around the pub.

His mobile vibrated in his pocket. The caller ID read: Ama Olakunbi. Why would Ama be calling? Too loud to take the call, he edged through the crowds to get outside, dodging hugs and shoulder rubs from intoxicated strangers.

'Hey, Ama. How are you?'

'Oh.' Clear delight in her expression. 'Wonderful. Absolutely wonderful! We could get used to this, you know. All your white tablecloths and fancy Champagne.' She joked in her steady, warm-hearted voice.

'Get used to it! This is only the beginning. The hard work is finally paying off. Soon it will be Champagne for breakfast.'

Ama's laughter was infectious.

'Not sure how that'll go down on the estate, but I'm willing to try it.' Even more endearing as she continued her own joke, but then she switched to a more serious tone.

'I'm proud of you, Grayson. *Adidas* sponsorship, it's a big deal.'

'It wasn't me Ama. It was all Joel. He does the hard bit. I'm just his representative, you know.'

'Well,' she said, 'he does, but you know you are more than that to him. You have always worked well together.'

'Thanks Ama, but it was all you and Kamsi. You were there from the start,'

He rarely got emotional. How many had he had?

'You were there for both of us.'

Ama would always express her feelings. He never could, but something in the way she spoke encouraged him to. He adored her for this. With anyone else, he kept his emotions under lock and key. Maybe it was the Christmas spirit, or the uplifting sound of Ama's voice, but watching the joyful strangers spill out of the pub door into the falling snow, he drifted to thoughts of those dear to him, Joel, Kamsi, Ama, Estella and inevitably, his mother.

He only had one genuine memory of his mother, but it was a joyful one. They were playing Guess Who together at the kitchen table, both pulling faces to mimic the characters. The hysterical laughter, the happiness. So full of life. It was how he wanted to remember her. The small amount of good in his life, he attributed to her. He loved the memory, but hated the pain as it faded.

'Speaking of his Lordship.' Ama broke the moment's silence.

'You can tell him we got home just fine. That we loved the dinner and wished he had stayed for dessert, but we know he deserves to celebrate. You youngsters have a little more energy than us.'

The statement came as a shock. He had assumed Joel

would still be with Ama and Kamsi, who were never ones to call an early end to a social gathering.

'I'll tell him.'

It was second nature to cover for him. He had been doing it all his life.

In high spirits, her voice like a Baptist choir lifted the soul.

Rounded off with more of that infectious laughter as she pushed her joke for a second time.

'We'll see him on Sunday, or next week at the Community Centre. Assuming his Lordship still remembers where it is.'

Grayson hadn't laughed along, but she hadn't seemed to notice.

Where is he?

The anxiety returned.

The deal signed at three o'clock at the rep's office in Soho. They went straight to *Smith & Wollensky's* in the *Adelphi* for Champagne at four. He had made a weak excuse and left shortly after. Quietly telling Ama and Kamsi he would go to see Estella. Even though he had not made plans to see her until later that evening. They would understand, but also knew it would also annoy Joel no end, abandoning such an important occasion.

Joel wasn't a fan of Estella. She didn't like Joel much either. Perhaps that was the source of Grayson's anxiety. Ever since she and Grayson got close, she would barely acknowledge Joel's existence. If she did, it would usually be an indirect slight about how Grayson was not spending enough time with her, as if to suggest Joel was a burden on his life. Sure, Joel had led them into some unpleasant situations here and there over the years, but she refused to see his good side, even though she knew everything he and his aunties had done for Grayson.

He snapped from the thought back to the issue at hand. They would have been eating by five at the latest. Joel must have left no later than seven. Over four hours ago.

His sigh froze in the frigid, Fitzrovia air. The evening was about to get a little more complicated.

The easiest way to St James's Street was to take a taxi from Langham Place. With the traffic, it would take the same time to pace down there, but at least in a taxi, he would have the time to gather his thoughts. He slid his phone back into his pocket; darted down Little Riding House Street, emerging under the glow of the *All Saints' Church*. He crossed the street to jump into a taxi sat at the stand at the *Langham Hotel*.

As the taxi crawled down Regent Street, Grayson could not help but remember the day they met. Four days after his mother lost her battle with cancer and his world fell apart, six-year-old Grayson Day was given a small piece of solace. He was given a best friend. He was given Joel Olakunbi. Now twenty-two years later, he knew his best friend was in trouble.

4 PAIR

♠♠♠

'Dad!'

'Dad! Dad, wake up!' He pleaded and pulled at his arm, but there was no response.

'Please dad, wake up!' Desperation had long since set in.

He could no longer see. Non-stop tears streaming down his face, everything was blurry. His lungs hurt. He struggled to breathe as he pleaded with the lifeless body for a reaction. Again tugging on his arm, as hard as he could.

He needed him to wake up. He needed his dad to tell him it would be ok.

Mum was never coming home. She was supposed to. She had missed his sixth birthday. The doctors were supposed to make her better. *Why didn't they make her better?* They had told him she would come home and be his mum again. He needed his mum.

It seemed like an eternity, now exhausted he fell to the floor beside the sofa, surrounded by empty cans and glass bottles. He couldn't remember ever being so hungry. He cried, until there were no tears left. His dad had been asleep on the sofa for days. And had cried, more than he ever could.

There was a noise.

The front gate swung open, someone was coming.

He shot up to the top of the stairs. That was the safest place. From there, he could see the front door as it opened.

Scared, he sat with his knees wrapped in his arms, rocking back and forth on the top step. Nurse Ama emerged at the bottom of the stairs. She called to him, but he would not move or answer.

'It's ok,' she whispered, 'it's ok.'

They were the same simple words she had said to him at the hospital, as she held him tight and wept with him in the moments following his mums's passing.

After a second plea for Grayson to come down, she made her way up.

'Whilst daddy sleeps, we will go out. I have someone for you to meet and play with.'

He didn't want to leave, but it frightened him to stay. Although he was there on the sofa, his dad was absent, lost, he had barely muttered a word in days. Grayson was alone, abandoned. He longed to go back to their daily routine. He needed someone. Ama was nice. She was a nurse at the hospital and she lived close to them, over on the *Cranbrook Estate*. Every now and then, she had got on the bus home with him and his dad. The number 48. He liked her Ama a lot. He had even drawn her in his family picture. He liked her voice. It was deep, calm and kind.

She passed him his trainers. As he laced them up, she cleared the bottles from the lounge to the kitchen and placed a glass of water next to his dad. She turned off the television and stuck to it a note. *'Niall, Grayson is at Kamsi's. I'll bring him back later. Ama'*. Once conscious, his dad would understand the message. Kamsiyonna was Ama's sister who lived with her on the *Cranbrook Estate*. Ama spoke about her a lot. She ran the Community Centre, which the residents called 'Kamsi's, an affectionate recognition of the energy and spirit she brought to the place.

Grayson reached up an held Ama's hand as they walked along the street. Although silent, his imagination was running wild. He was excited there would be someone new to play with. Since leaving the hospital a few days earlier, he had never felt so alone. During the time his mum had been in the hospital, his dad was there with him every second. They ate together, played games in the garden and sat side-by-side watching TV until bedtime. He found it hard to comprehend that his mum would never come home, but could not understand why his dad wouldn't look at him, talk to him, or play with him.

Grayson and Ama approached a small hexagonal brick building over on Mace Street, sitting in the shadows of one of the looming residential towers. He shivered. Ama stopped, reached down and straightened his jacket.

'Look Grayson, there it is. Kamsi's.'

Her wide smile eased his nerves.

'I know it looks scary from the outside, but inside there are high ceilings and bright colours. It's really fun. I promise. Last year my sister and a group of the residents, bought some paint, rollers and brushes. They spent a week painting it and making it lovely. You'll see. I'm very proud of her you know, we had lots of people from all over the estate come to help. It was like a party.'

As they stepped inside, Ama reached for another door. She pushed it open to reveal the main hall. It was light and bright, just as she had promised.

Kamsi greeted them with a soft smile. She was sitting at a table. As they walked over towards her, she stood and then squatted to Grayson's height.

'Hi Grayson,' a softness to her voice, 'my name is Kamsi, I am Ama's little sister.' She peered up at Ama with a small grin of admiration.

Too distracted to listen, Grayson peered beyond Kamsi to a small boy of a similar age. The boy was playing with a deck of cards laid out in front of him.

Joel peered up from the table and gave Grayson a wide smile, proudly showing his missing front teeth. Amused by this, Grayson was immediately comforted. It was the first time he had smiled since leaving the hospital.

Kamsi pulled out a chair for Grayson to sit and took off his hat and jacket. As he climbed onto the chair, Joel started to explain the game.

'It's called Cheat,' he said with excitement, 'you put down cards like this, say what you are putting down and I have to guess if you are cheating or not.'

The enthusiastic delivery and laughter had captivated Grayson.

'I know it!' He said. 'Me and my dad play it all the time. I always win.'

He picked up some cards and began to place them face-down, announcing to Joel what cards he had laid.

Kamsi looked across to Ama.

'How was Niall?'

'The same. We need to look out for the boy. He is OK with you here?'

'Grayson?' Kamsi called, drawing his attention away from the table of cards. Are you having fun?'

'Yes, its's my favourite game!' He said with a wide grin.
The sister's eyes met with a soft understanding smile.
'He'll be OK with us, for a while.'

♠♠♠

5 FOLD

50 St James's Street, St James's, SW1

30 November 2017

The bright lights of Piccadilly broke Grayson from the memory. A best friend, he scoffed. He was now a grown man; *should he need a babysitter? Told how to look after his money?* We all have our own issues to deal with. As he stewed on a moment of anger, he began to grapple with a shameful realisation that had been dragging on his subconscious. A realisation that he had seen addiction destroy his father. He knew the damage that it could do, yet he had stood by and watched his best friend slip deeper and deeper into his addiction. He considered the change in Joel over the last couple of years. Fuelled by depression, it had brought a carelessness to his actions. If unchecked, it could derail his boxing career, their business partnership, and perhaps even their friendship.

Joel continued to work hard at his craft, studying, dieting, and training. He was still unbeaten as a professional, but the term 'professional' was an insult to the occupation. Promoters and middlemen stripped the small *purses* he won. Once they had taken their cut, the reality for Joel was it would have been more lucrative to have stayed an amateur and sign-on at the local job centre.

He had done nothing to help, Grayson considered in shame. It was worse, he had been enabling him to function this way. The guilt swelled in his gut. When he had no one, Joel and his aunties had saved him, given him hope. When he was too young to understand.

Why had he not helped Joel earlier? Why did he leave his best friend to deal with this addiction alone? Why did he leave him behind?

The last question gnawed at him. Grayson's move to the West End four years earlier had put not only a geographical distance between them, but an emotional one. He enjoyed living there, but with the extortionate rent, he wondered if he only kept their business going to afford the lifestyle, rather than to continue to build something with his best friend.

Grayson and Joel had been running their business for close to ten years. They arranged private poker games. Their partnership was simple. Joel ran player background and security. Grayson ran venue selection and the game itself. They split the profits fifty-fifty. As they had done with every money-making scheme since their schooldays. What had started as a small-stakes cash-game to fill the demand from a few degenerates following the closure of the *Gutshot Club*, had now morphed into an invitation-only, three table game with much higher-stakes. With the higher stakes had come the greater reward, which afforded Grayson his West End lifestyle. Joel on the other hand, had stayed out East, close to his aunties, the majority of his earnings going towards nutrition and training.

His thoughts shifted back to the decisive moment. He should have stayed at the lunch. If he had stayed Joel would never have gone to the casino. He had left him in a place where it was easy for him to make excuses, leave the lunch and scratch the addictive itch that had progressively worsened. In hindsight it seemed obvious, but he was too caught up in his drama with Estella to see it.

Joel had no choice when he took that first boxing purse, he and his aunties desperately needed the money. The hospital had cut Ama's hours and Kamsi's salary at the Community Centre was minimal. That first purse was just two thousand pounds, with no win bonus. The cost, however, was far greater. With that payment, he had turned professional. He had to step aside from the Team GB Academy and give up on his dream of becoming an Olympian. At first Joel coped well with the disappointment, but seeing lesser fighters go on to fame and glory, as he reached his late twenties, more and more Joel felt like he had missed his moment. Had never had a real shot. A real chance to win a sizeable purse.

Grayson remembered sitting with Joel to watch the boxing at the Beijing Olympics. The very competition that he should have been working towards. It was excruciating to witness Joel bury the regret as deep as possible. Made all the worse when a British fighter, who Joel had beat as a youth, went on to win a medal. He tried hard to mask the disappointment, but Grayson knew it devastated him much more than he would admit, much more than he could handle. He should have done more to support Joel in his hour of need.

Since that point Joel had spent more and more time at the poker tables. His play was strong enough to handle the small-stakes games in the East End. A hard grind for small returns. There at least, every bet meant something to the mid-management white-collared players sitting opposite. Their reactions were true, Joel could read them, play correct strategy and thrive.

The high stakes rooms in the West End were a different kettle-of-fish. Grayson knew this all too well. Even with his advanced game he chose not to venture into the lion's den too often. The players there did not even blink at the money they wagered. Oligarchs, Asian businessmen, professional footballers, most were killing time, the money meant nothing to them. Their play was erratic, unpredictable. A skill game descended into luck. They could chew you up, take all your money and not even notice you were there.

The taxi pulled up at a building sat proudly at the top end of St James's Street. Grayson exited and removed his jacket as he mounted the stairs of the large townhouse three at a time. The grandeur of the detailed exterior stone work was surpassed only by the impressive triple height interior. The foyer had an unforgiving marble floor, lavish furnishings, and scented candles which flowed through to the ballroom. A symphony of poker and blackjack chips clicking accentuated an energetic buzz of laughter. He hoped he was not too late and could talk Joel out of playing on. Perhaps convince him to recommence the celebrations and head out to a bar in Soho or something.

A jolt of anxiety hit Grayson when he crossed the threshold. Searching for his friend, he rushed across the foyer passed the decadent bar room to the right, where out of the corner of his eye he saw Debora behind the marble counter. A Brazilian girl who had picked up the bar work using a fake Spanish identification, stating that she had been born in Malaga. She had laughed when she told Grayson a couple of months earlier, suggesting that a Portuguese document would have been much more suitable to her native tongue, but she used her mesmeric smile and mouthed a soft 'hola' to the club manager who took a cursory glance at the document before offering the prime shifts on the rota. The best evenings for picking up tips.

Since starting at the casino earlier that year, Debora had taken quite a shine to him and had not been shy in letting him know. The more he resisted, the more blatant she became. She seemed to enjoy the challenge. She was certainly stunning to look at. And no doubt kind and fun, but her advances brought out a nervous tension in him. An insecurity exposed by anyone who tried to get close. He kept his inner-circle small. He was comfortable that way. The only girl he wanted was Estella, but he had even managed to push her away.

Debora was pouring a drink for an elegantly dressed Asian woman sitting on a stool in front of her. Detecting the motion she looked up. Her face immediately turned to concern as her focus moved to the main ball room in front of him.

As he walked in, he scanned the vast space, centring in on the room at the rear where they played the high stakes poker. He stopped in his tracks. On the sofa in front of the room was Joel sat head-in-hands. He wasn't a man mid-way through a poker game. It was a man broken. One that had clearly been on-tilt and lost more than he could afford. On-tilt, when all reason, rational and strategy goes out of the window. Carrying the emotions of the last hand into the next. A complete loss of control. Taking greater risks, playing poorer hands. With the stubbornness Joel possessed, Grayson knew there would have been no stopping him.

Debora appeared at his side, she reached and grasped his hand.

'Grayson. Don't!...' A shake of her head pleaded with him, her long dark hair swayed, exposing the small spade tattoo on her neck. Her eyes met his. His look urged her for more.

'It's over Grayson. Thirty thousand. It's over.'

'Shit!'

He brought his hands to his face, pulled down on his jaw as he took in what she was saying. That was the full amount of Joel's first retainer payment from *Adidas Boxing*.

'I'm sorry.' She said, her eyes heavy with concern.

Grayson again stared over towards the sofa. He had expected some bad news, perhaps Joel would have been down a couple of thousand, but losing thirty-thousand was beyond his fears.

How had it got to this? He had barely had that money for half a day. Disappointment devolved into anger. His neck stiff, back aching. He realised that he hadn't been doing the heavy lifting in their friendship, as he'd thought. He had been carrying the guilt of leaving his friend to fight a battle he was losing. He was more than his friend, he was a business partner, he was his brother, but he was lost.

Friendships, like the cards dealt to you. You decide when to stick with them and fight it out or when to fold and walk away.

Fight it out or fold?

That was the decision Grayson Day now faced with Joel Olakunbi.

Fight it out or fold?

He put his jacket on and walked out of the door, back into the damp December evening.

6 OUTS

REPTON BOXING CLUB, 116 CHESHIRE ST, BETHNAL GREEN, E2

3 DECEMBER 2017

Frost clung to the murky East End air as Grayson pulled open the heavy iron gate. The sun was still an hour or two from rising and only his footsteps on the gravel dared break the Sunday morning silence.

There were no signs of life coming from the former Victorian Bathhouse. Grayson wondered if his intuition had failed him this time, but as he unlatched the entrance door, inhaling the distinctive liniment oils and sharp smelling *Deep Heat,* he heard slapping of leather gloves on leather bag coming from the back corner of the gym. The powerful sound of punches and the releasing of anger.

Since walking through the door as a sixteen-year-old, *Repton Boxing Club* had become a second home to Joel Olakunbi. Although a relative late-comer to boxing, the trainers noticed that he had a God-given talent. His reflexes quicker and power greater than any youth-level fighter in the club. But it was his ability to read and second guess his opponents that impressed them the most. He had instinctive reactions and lightning quick speed. He respected the structure and intense routine they put him on, working with specialists every weekday on weights, cardio, agility and sparring.

Sunday morning, however was *his* time. Additional hours he put in above and beyond requirement. A work rate that his competitors could not match. Every Sunday morning, before showering and meeting his aunties for Mass, he would train alone. Alone with his dedication. Alone with his thoughts. Alone in the cold dark gym, just him and the moonlit bags hanging from the rafters. It was *his* time. On this Sunday morning, he would be alone with his thoughts, alone with his fears. And alone with his sins.

It was a confession that Grayson wanted from his friend, but he would not lead him to it. Joel would have to come clean on his own. Their friendship may endure. It would take more than money to break that, but if their business partnership was to survive, Joel would need to have the strength to admit the events of Friday night. Grayson needed no explanation, only the reassurance of trust.

He knew that the addiction was now too strong. Joel had passed a point. It was inevitable that from now everything he earned in the ring or from the business would be lost at the poker tables. Worse still, that sponsorship money was supposed to have gone towards the preparation for his title fight. He needed specialised training, medical and nutritional support. He needed to pay his team for their additional time. Where would Joel get that money from now?

He entered through a white tiled archway, a sign that read *'No Guts, No Glory'* hung overhead. Across the hall, he studied the powerful lineation of his friend. His smooth dark skin tone incandescent against the matt-black *Adidas* ath-leisure wear shaped tight to his sculpted frame. He skirted his way around the raised ring, the central feature of the main hall, onerously lit by the moon through the skylight above. As he approached and leaned against the wall, Joel continued to work the bag. From first sight of his sweat-stained top, it was clear he had been at it for a while.

'I'd hate to know what he did to you.'

'He might have snuck up on me, in the Godforsaken hours of the morning.' Joel neither looked up, nor broke rhythm in his punches.

'Now, now. Blasphemy will not be well received. Especially on a Sunday.'

'Well, blasphemy can fuck-off, if it wants to disturb me when I'm working.'

Joel took one final hard hook shot to the bag, a head-level knockout punch, before looking up to Grayson and breaking into a smile. It was the same smile the six-year-old Joel gave him, only now matured by sculpted stubble, adding excessive definition to an already strong jaw. Innocence, replaced by honed charisma. Although Grayson couldn't help but notice a flickering of guilt in his eyes.

'All right Fam? What you doing up at this hour? And at these Ends?

'Thought I would come by,' he gestured to the *Adidas Boxing* logo on Joel's chest, 'you know, make sure fame and fortune hadn't gone to your head.' With a grin, Grayson sized up Joel's head through thumb and forefinger.

'Mind you, that is a big head.'

'That ain't me Bruv. You know that. It's all business now. So no need to worry. You can focus your attention on Estella. Sure she would appreciate that. How is she by the way?'

The bitterness to his sarcasm made it clear to Grayson that

Ama and Kamsi had let slip the reason for him leaving the lunch.

'She's out of the picture now.' Grayson said. Joel rolled his eyes.

'I decided I needed a break. You know, put my efforts into making sure you're ready for the fight, but I thought I'd have seen you on Friday night?'

'Ha. Nah, the dinner ran late, Am and Kam were on it. You know.' Joel forced a single syllable laugh. 'By the time we finished up, I was shattered Fam. That was a long day.' He concluded.

Grayson detected pain in Joel's voice. He had hoped for a different response and a different outcome. He couldn't help feel for his friend as he struggled to get through the entire lie.

'Fair enough fella.'

He would not call him out. Not here, not now. He played along to close off the subject. Joel's cover-up had helped him justify a decision he had made before walking into the gym that morning. In reality, he had made it before leaving the casino on Friday night. It was time to cut Joel out of their business, out of the next game. For his own good. If he was out of the business he would have no access to cash to gamble away. He could focus on the boxing and make sure he won his upcoming title fight.

It would be for Joel's own good, but Grayson knew he would have to deceive his friend to pull it off. And that such deceit brought with it risk. Joel would not see it that way.

Grayson was confident he could handle it alone, perhaps even put aside Joel's share and put right the money he had lost. It was a chance to thank him for the support Joel had shown him over the years. He knew in reality it would be a payment that may help him shed the guilt of letting his friend slip deeper into addiction.

'It's been a long journey, but you've got your shot.'

'A journey?' Joel rolled his eyes as he threw a high-right glancing jab to the bag. 'Whatever you want to call it.'

A journey to Joel was an ironic reference, rarely having left London. Most of his fights had been at *York Hall*, a stone's throw away from where they stood. On big fight nights they could hear the crowd from the *Cranbrook Estate*.

He had moved out from his aunties' apartment, but wishing to stay close to them, the gym and having limited funds, he had rented a rundown studio apartment above a nail salon on Roman Road. Grayson, however was thinking about the journey more in the philosophical context.

'Come on, I still remember your first punch.'

'Yeah. Always getting your arse out of trouble.'

The pair laughed as they both recalled the fateful day at *Morpeth Secondary School* when Joel threw the punch that signified the first step in his boxing career.

'Lloyd fucking Blake. That boy never learned his lesson.' Joel rolled his eyes, letting out a small chuckle through a wide smile.

Grayson joined him with a subtle shaking of the head.

'You're all on track for the fight? Anything you need?'

'I'm all good cheers. Always more work to be done.'

'Well, I'll let you get back to your craft then.'

'Cheers for stopping by. You'll be at Kamsi's on Wednesday?'

'I'll be there. See you then.'

As he turned towards the entrance, the sound of leather on leather restarted. Grayson couldn't help but think the punches were softer. Lying and covering up the Friday night loss had sapped the strength from Joel's arms. Either that or relief, thinking his lie had been bought.

As he stepped outside, Grayson reached for his phone, typed and sent the same message to two very different recipients.

'Friday night is on. Meet tomorrow as discussed.'

7 CRACK

SUMMER 2005

♠♠♠

Until the fight, the profit from their playground enterprises had kept Grayson and Joel in the latest *Air Max* trainers. Each twenty pack of *Benson* or *Marlboro Lights* cigarettes they sold would net a pound profit, *Clipper* lighters the same. Every now and again they would look for ways to improve their profit margin, but the real money spinner was the simple dice-game they had setup in the passageway behind the bike sheds. Six students would each put two pounds down, roll a die and the winner took away a crisp ten-pound note. Two pounds went to the 'organisers' for controlling the game and running a few sets of eyes to alert them of any teachers prowling the area.

Grayson would be in charge of the game and Joel the security. They had realised that many students would gamble their pocket money for some illicit lunchtime excitement. It was more enjoyable than the mile round trip to the chip shop. They facilitated the game with the simple task of keeping a steady, but not conspicuous stream of punters circulating the playground. And at the end of each day, they swapped out a rucksack of pound coins for notes. The local corner shop owner was always keen to oblige, for a small fee. They would change the shops every now and again, so as not to raise suspicion.

Across various schemes, Grayson and Joel had been netting decent pocket money since beginning Year Nine. In Year Eleven, amongst the oldest students in the school, threat levels were lower and profits had soared to a hundred quid a week each. A decent bit of cash for a pair of sixteen-year-olds.

The increased activity had not gone unnoticed. One day in late February, when mock GCSE exams had disturbed the usual lunchtime routine, Lloyd Blake, a pale-faced red-headed shit-bag, who also lived on the *Cranbrook Estate*, brought the Walsh brothers on to the school grounds.

The Walsh brothers, at seventeen and eighteen, were too old for school. In any case, it had been a long time since they had graced the *Morpeth* playground with their presence. The older brother expelled in Year Ten and the younger barely attending since.

Lloyd strolled up to Grayson, the two bulky goons in tow. He attempted to snatch the backpack, but Grayson did not release it. The two wrestled back and forth, Grayson tucked it low to his gut forcing Lloyd to bend forward to rip it from him. As he did so, Joel came running into the passageway from his lookout position, moving towards the skirmish, breaking through the outstretched arms of the Walsh brothers. He sent his momentum forward, planted his left foot and from a high angle of trajectory, swung a right hook down towards Lloyd's jaw. The punch connected sending Lloyd to the ground and his cheekbone across his face.

A sharp cracking sound of Lloyd's jaw and cheekbone breaking brought an immediate end to the fight. The Walsh brothers backed off, whilst Joel stood over Lloyd, snarling down towards him. Shock of his own strike stunned him, but his fist remained clenched and shoulder cocked.

A code of silence had held around the dice game, but the news of the fight soon reached the teachers, as had the identity of who had thrown the punch that had hospitalised Lloyd Blake. As an average student, they didn't consider the circumstances before expelling Joel just months before his final exams. It had devastated his aunties. Not long after, they marched him into the *Repton Boxing Club*, hoping that the trainers there could install some father-figure-like discipline to the boy.

8 BIG SLICK

4 DECEMBER 2017

As James Johnson pushed through the door, the high-pitched ring of the bell mustered an acknowledging nod from the owner behind the counter. All other customers were too deep in discussion for distraction. Saturday's injury-time defeat had stirred up the same old debate, and it had raged on ever since. The *Upton Park* faithful voicing fierce regret at having left the old ground for the *London Stadium*. 'It's just not us! There's no atmosphere! It's affecting performance!' From the six AM opening, opinions in the *Arches Cafe* on Three Colts Lane had been flying. 'We need to modernise. If we would ever be a big club, we needed a big stadium.' A battle land aroma of fried bacon and filtered coffee.

As the big lad threaded his twenty stone mass through the fixed tables and chairs,   his long black *Stone Island* jacket dragged across half the tables as he passed. At the back of the cafe, an empty seat was being saved for him.

'Bit lively in here for a Monday morning Bruv?' He squeezed one leg under the table, 'surprised to get a call from you. Thought Morgan's crew handled your security?'

Grayson had little time for pleasantries. He preferred repetition and didn't like change. The break from routine had him on edge. He had to get used to the fact that Joel would not be at Friday's game.

'Listen.' He said with impatience. 'I called you because I need a new crew for Friday night.' He stared at Johnson to make sure he had his full attention.

'One on-the-door. Two inside. 8 o'clock. It will be a local location, confirmed sometime later today.'

'Got it.' Johnson said, with a respectful but mocking serious acknowledgement. After a moments' pause, while the cogs turned, he continued.

'How much P gonna be in the room?'

'About 180 thou. The winner might need an escort home.'

The amount clearly surprised Johnson. He nodded his thick-tied dreads and made teeth-drying gestures in approval towards the business level that this once quiet little card game had now reached.

'Tools?'

'Punters get a respectful shakedown, but they shouldn't be carrying.'

'And us?'

'As you see fit, but nothing heavy,' Grayson asserted. 'We consider it a gentlemanly game.'

'All right Fam. All good. Drop me the deets.'

As James stood to leave, Grayson added.

'And, don't talk about this around the estate.'

'I get it bruv. It's on the QT.'

Up until this point the thought of going behind Joel's back

had been just that, a thought.

He had now crystallised it. Unease set in.

As Johnson left the cafe, clumsily squeezing through the tables, Grayson took a moment to run through the scene he saw in the casino Friday night. Then he ran through his interaction with Joel at the Boxing Club on Sunday morning. He reassured himself. He was making the right call. Joel needs to focus on boxing.

Catching the eye of the owner.

'I'll grab the bill mate. Cheers.'

9 CONNECTOR

Repetition and routine. Most *Underground* commuters, consciously or not, get on the most efficient tube carriage for their exit. Years of repetition and routine lead them to the same spot on the platform every morning and every evening. Avoiding the rush hour push and saving precious minutes on their daily journey to and from work.

Such observations gave Grayson a sense of comfort, even if his tube travel was infrequent. Anxiety would fade as he ran through the calculations, at times verbalising the station names as he gathered control of his breathing. Estella had once referred to his behaviour as endearingly 'spectrumy'. Within hours of getting his first payout from the business and leasing his rented Fitzrovia apartment, a moments walk from Oxford Circus tube station, he had committed to memory every scenario, for every station on the Central, Victoria and Bakerloo lines. He was compiling inane information that rarely yielded any benefit, but better he thought than wasting his time reading tabloid gossip and posting opinions on social media. That was a senseless waste of brain capacity.

Although his position was of no real consequence, when he reached the far right of the Bethnal Green Central Line platform and realised he was in the wrong spot for his exit. He took it as an indicator of a much deeper distraction.

He was uncomfortable, nervous even. For the first time in his life he was deliberately excluding Joel, not only from the game but from the partnership and from his trust. He knew it wouldn't be easy. He relied on Joel to bring a calmness to their work. He provided a confidence and physical presence towards any situation they had faced over the years. They had had very limited trouble on the estate and had successfully avoided the gangs throughout their youth. He didn't like the unease of not having him by his side.

For Bond Street, he should have gone to carriage six. He peered up at the board. With two minutes to the train's arrival and a packed platform, the push back to carriage six wasn't worth it. He would exit at Oxford Circus and walk the extra five minutes to Brook Street Mews. He didn't like to be late, but given it was Piers Fitzgerald-Smithe who was waiting for him, he figured it would be five minutes less that he had to endure his special brand of Etonian arrogance.

Piers was certainly from the opposite end of society. A purebred with a hollow sense of privilege and old money. A product of parents that loved him so much, they packed him off to boarding school at age six. Grayson, born and raised on an estate in the East End, figured the only thing they had in common was the lack of parentage. He didn't dislike Piers, he was just hard work, but it was important to keep him on-side. He needed him for what he had planned.

Grayson had known Piers for a little over a year. He had found him after their last location provider let them down. Joel referred to it as 'his friendship of necessity', having never met Piers himself. He would often joke that based on how Grayson described him, temptation may be too strong to 'knock the posh dickhead out, just for fun.' So he left all interactions with him down to Grayson.

Piers was the type who wanted to get ahead, but felt that others needed to do the hard work to propel him. The chip on his shoulder drove him to rebel. Perhaps another reason he had 'outside of the club' acquaintances such as Grayson. He was uncomfortable stepping into his father's well worn brogues. He wanted to show him he didn't need the allowance that still hit his account like clockwork every month. Of course, he still spent it, but it was a frustrating reminder of the cheques he had received at school to pass on to the administrative office for fees and board. The only form of correspondence with his father. Grayson knew all to well what it was to have little to no connection with a father, Niall's reliance on alcohol having grown progressively worse over the years.

On this occasion, it was Grayson that needed the favour, so they were meeting on Piers' turf, a little artesian coffee shop tucked away in a picturesque mews behind *Claridges*. Piers could often be found there, entertaining colleagues and clients in his obnoxious manner. Grayson didn't mind the choice, the staff were friendly and although he knew little about the intricacies of coffee making, he appreciated that there, it tasted good.

Piers, or 'Two-Dads' as most in the market called him in ridicule of his double barrelled surname, was a commercial estate agent who specialised in what he called 'Fringe Areas' or 'London Unlimited' when selling the East End postcodes to new media and tech start-ups, who had long been priced out of their traditional office locations in Soho and Covent Garden.

Public schoolboys riddled the commercial real estate market. Living in their parents' SW1 apartments, paying bills with an allowance rather than salary. Piers was one such boy, fresh out of University, red-brick of course. He dressed, spoke, and acted like he owned the two-bit three-name partnership for which he worked. His uncle had arranged the job. One partner was an old school chum. Nepotism at its finest. Although his brand of arrogance was abrasive to most, Grayson couldn't help but be both irritated and charmed in equal measure with the naivety Piers possessed. No real understanding of what it was like to live without privilege.

Clad in his pinstripe suit and floral patterned *Hermes* tie, Piers was conditioned to look down his nose as he strutted around the streets of the East End, commenting on the surrounds as if it was a game of *Monopoly* and he had a pocket full of cash having just passed *Go*. He revelled in the abuse hurled at him from white van drivers, snarky 'prawn-cocktail' comments from panel beaters and straight-to-his-face vitriol from tradesmen. Grayson almost admired his ability to rile people with no real reason. All the same, it was less aggravation to meet on the less hostile turf of the West End.

As Grayson arrived, Piers was sitting by the front window. An etched smirk on his long drawn horse-like face, the result of a few generations of inbreeding. His persona matched the greasiness of his hair. Never likely to win second place in a beauty contest, that was for sure.

As he entered, with a small grin of exertion, Grayson summoned the energy he would need for the meeting. Needs-must. Piers was a helpful connection to have. He was excitable, keen to illustrate that he knew it all. For a thousand quid cash and a small rogue taste of excitement in his otherwise textbook bourgeoisie life, Piers would happily arrange the keys to one of the disused buildings his firm managed and tell any security to have the night off.

'Morning chap.' Piers said as he stood. A dramatic hand-shaker. More wet-fish than firm.

'Not been to the office yet?' Grayson posed the question, whilst looking down at two empty coffee cups and a broad-sheet folded open to page 24.

'Flexible working is all the rage these days my boy.' The chuckle was confirmation that in his book, flexible working equated to doing sweet fuck-all for the first couple of hours of the day.

'Another?' Grayson gestured to the empty cups.

'Sure, a Cappuccino would be pleasurable.'

Grayson leaned towards the counter and placed the order before turning his attention back to Piers.

'So tell me old boy. Is there good bunce in the boxing game?'

Bunce. Where does Little Lord Fauntleroy pick up this shit? He was the antithesis of an East Ender, if ever there was one.

'Yes, Piers. Very good "bunce".' Grayson's sarcasm on full display.

'Seems so. Very subject de jour. Say's here that this Mayweather chap was paid over one-hundred million for fighting that McGregor fella. He's one of yours isn't he?'

'What do you mean, one of mine?' Grayson said genuinely perplexed.

'Irish. You are from Irish descendancy, are you not?'

'Well, if you mean is my dad Irish? Then yes, but I've never been there, don't want to go there and don't sound Irish, do I?.'

'Fair point.'

'Plus my mum was Finnish.'

'A real mongrel aren't you.' Piers laughed.

'Whatever. Look Piers. Can we get on to business?'

Piers responded with a smirk.

'The *Cranbrook* issue we discussed last month? Because I've got no further intel, I'm afraid. Haven't seen old Sloaney in bloody ages. He works far too hard.'

'No. This week's venue.' Grayson said, impatience growing. 'Do you have a place for Friday?'

'For you Sir, I have the perfect asset.'

'Do tell.' He couldn't help but jest at the pretentiousness of Piers.

'In your favourite neighbourhood. Do you know the old *Acorn* pub on the Queensbridge Road?' He didn't wait for an answer. 'We took over management last week. Yet to place security.'

A pretty, short-haired waitress with neck tattoos and a range of facial piercings placed the coffees and two slices of warm banana bread in front of them. She shot Grayson a smile as she turned back to the counter.

Transfixed, Piers joked, 'I don't think mother would approve.'

'You have the keys?' Said Grayson, switching to a more serious tone.

Piers slid an envelope across the table.

'Alarm codes are also in there. Be a good chap and lock up when your done.'

To indulge Piers in his need for theatre, Grayson also slid an envelope across the table. His contained a thousand pounds. He kept his hand held firm on the envelope and locked eyes with Piers.

'Now,' he said with a smile, 'I do need an additional favour.'

10   COMMUNITY POT

CRANBROOK ESTATE COMMUNITY CENTRE, BETHNAL GREEN, E2

6 DECEMBER 2017

Arriving early to lend a hand, it surprised Grayson to see the chairs unstacked and already set out uniformly across the main hall of the *Cranbrook Community Centre*. On a table by the wall, biscuits, crisps and a warming tea urn were awaiting the Estate residents. The sisters were ready. Ama seated in the front row, looking up intently at Kamsi, who was standing, rehearsing her opening remarks. Kamsi always carried a sadness in her eyes. On a one-to-one level, it gave her a deep sense of empathy and connection. Grayson hoped the same would be true when she addressed the residents that evening. She cared for their wellbeing and deserved their attention. Wearing a turquoise *Gele* headdress and colour coordinated *Buba* blouse she looked calm, confident, and prepared.

On more than a few occasions over the years, Grayson wondered why neither Kamsi, nor Ama had found a man and settled down. It was not like they hadn't received offers. It was moments like this however, he could see their devotion to each other and their community left no room for men. He was happy that there was room for Joel and grateful there was space for him. He too thought of them as his aunties, perhaps even surrogate mothers. As Grayson watched them debate talking points back and forth, he couldn't help but think the closeness of their relationship had been a positive influence on his friendship with Joel.

With a wave and accompanying smile, Grayson walked to the back of the hall where Joel was moving old gym mats to make way for more chairs. Perhaps now, in the company of his aunties, there may be some sign of remorse. Or at the very least he might show to Grayson that he needed his friend to confide in. No, only a smile and three-fingered salute. His armour of charisma not even pierced. Grayson masked his frustration and determined there was no need for words. All that could be said for now, had been said on Sunday, in the pre-dawn darkness of the *Repton Boxing Club*.

The flyers and general chatter around the estate had created quite a buzz around today's meeting. They were expecting a large turnout. Many of the residents were unaware of the threat encroaching on them. The information that Kamsi and her volunteers had spread had travelled fast and caused quite an uproar. Once awoken, Kamsi knew that there would be some strong, if not eloquently delivered opinions.

The first group arrived fifteen minutes early, followed by a constant stream entering the hall. Whilst Kamsi and Ama did their best to keep the pre-meeting chatter social, Grayson and Joel circulated the room handing out refreshments and making sure the elder guests had their tea mugs topped up.

As 7.30pm rolled around, Kamsi stepped up to the makeshift stage, as the residents continued to courteously swap and shuffle chairs. The elder ladies being granted the premium seating, equidistant from the stage and the array of home-baked goods that had now overrun the side table. Making sure the recipients knew who baked each cake would be high on their agenda. They packed the hall to the rafters, standing room only against the side walls.

Kamsi scanned the room as if to check the attendance of the most active members of the community. Each in turn offered a look of encouragement and support. She took a second. Embraced the moment. A multi-cultural, multi-religious gathering. An ethnicity mix of predominantly Bangladeshi, Black and White. The Black community on the estate was pretty evenly split between those of Caribbean descent and those like Ama and Kamsi, of African heritage.

'Bawo ni!'

She began, a little jittery at first. She had never spoken to so many people at once.

'Hello friends, neighbours. Thank you for coming.'

Grayson hoped that Kamsi would soon slip into her engaging ways, but looking around the room, he felt a growing anxiety. Some residents wanted to skip the niceties and get straight to the point: *Tower Hamlets Council* selling the *Cranbrook Estate*.

'We know you are all concerned and will no doubt have questions.' She looked down at her notes in a controlled manner, and then continued.

'We will first...'

A shout from the back of the hall interrupted her mid-sentence.

'What about our homes?!'

'Where will we live?' Another voice shouted.

Chatter around the hall began to bubble, volume increased

as whispers turned to debate.

Tension had been growing on the estate for several months in the wake of the *Grenfell Tower* disaster. According to official statements, seventy-two people had lost their lives and at least seventy others were injured as fire engulfed the building, trapping residents inside. Speculation was rife and many across London, especially in the fringe communities, believed the numbers were much higher, being lessened by the authorities to reduce the risk of civil unrest. The inadequacies of *Grenfell* had left every council in London rushing to audit the fire safety standards of their residential towers. On the *Cranbrook Estate* there had been a high number of inspections carried out by *Tower Hamlets Council*, but not a lot of questions answered.

'Ladies and gentlemen.' Kamsi tried to reengage the group, but to no avail.

'Ladies and gentlemen.'

Although a mid-size frame, her voice was soft and rarely had she had to raise it. She had worked hard to prepare her speech and to inform her community. Now it was all going to waste. Drowned out in non-constructive chatter.

By this point, her older sister Ama had had enough. She lifted her right leg up on to the stage and clambered up, turning and bellowing at the top of her lungs.

'For the love of God! Would you all please shut-up and listen! We ask for fifteen minutes, nothing more.'

The hall fell silent.

True to their ways, the sisters couldn't help but break into a smile and gentle laughter. Ama curtsied and waved Kamsi forward to recommence her speech. Grayson looked across to the back of the room where Joel was chuckling along with his aunties' soft laughter. It frustrated him that even having lost all of the money he had worked so hard to earn, Joel seemed not to have a care in the world. As if it was Grayson's job to carry the burden of concern.

Watching this unfold, admiring the women that had raised him, Grayson wished he could do more to help. He was, however, glad that he had got the ball rolling, having informed Kamsi of the back-channel discussions between *Tower Hamlets Council* and the West End Private Equity firms.

He had Piers Fitzgerald-Smithe to thank for the initial tip. 'Something quite literally up your *Strasse*.' That was how he phrased it. Some 'old mucker' of his had drank a few too many *Drambuies* at the *Bucks Club*. Whilst boasting about his hot-shot private equity career, he had spilt the beans about a large deal on the horizon. Piers, always one to stir the pot, had suggested that the 'new money try-hard needs to learn that loose-lips sink ships.' Grayson didn't pretend to understand the relationship between Piers and his so-called friend, but he was thankful for the information.

'Ladies and gentlemen. Thank you for your time this evening.' Kamsi continued with a new-found courage. She mouthed a 'thank you' to Ama and went on in a calm and simple manner to deliver her speech.

'Here are the facts as we understand them. *Tower Hamlets Council* have started discussions to sell the ownership and management of our estate. Any decision to do so will require a program of formal communication with the Tenants and Residents Association. Therefore, I am speaking from the perspective of a resident and on behalf only of the Community Centre.'

She took a breath and scanned the room. As her eyes met Grayson's he offered a smile and small fist pump of encouragement. Kamsi, and Ama for that matter, never failed to surprise him. They knew their people. From the moment they arrived twenty-five years earlier, having claimed asylum from religious persecution in Northern Nigeria, their kindness, positivity and goodwill had ingratiated them in the community and earned the trust of their neighbours.

Although the sisters rarely spoke about the bad times, as they called them. Over the years Grayson had pieced together the parts of the journey from their city of Kano to London's East End. On a Sunday in mid-October 1991, shortly after Ama had graduated medical studies at the *Bayero University*, the family had gathered for Mass. Their parents had asked the sisters to pop down to the *Yakura Market* and pick-up some vegetables for supper that evening. Over the prior days there had been religious unrest, as a Christian Reverend from Germany planned to visit the predominantly Muslim city, on what was termed a 'Modern Day Crusade'.

As they reached the market, there was a palpable tension in the air. Large groups of men gathered and blocked the sister's route home. They listened as the chants got louder and more aggressive, climaxing as the group set off Northwards, heading toward their neighbourhood.

Upon navigating their way back, the sisters found the rooms empty. They headed over to the *St Thomas Church* compound. That was where they found their parents, brother and his wife among the bodies and ruins. Never told explicitly, Grayson understood that a neighbour sat crying in the wreckage, holding Joel in her arms. Ama's grief manifested itself in a resilience she had never felt. She gathered her younger sister and nephew and fled west to Niamey in Niger, a week later boarding a flight to London.

The sisters had quickly become de facto leaders of the community. It was the residents themselves that had convinced Kamsi to take on the position as Community Centre Manager. Although she never used that title. At first, she was reluctant, shy, and fearful that her English language skills were not up-to-par, but when a resident nominated her at the Tenants and Residents Association's Meeting and eleven people stood to second her, she accepted, feeling not only emboldened, but inspired to put her heart and soul into the role. Today she stood in front of them trying with kid-gloves to deliver the damming news. This would be the first meeting of many. A precursor to battle. She wanted to ease them into it, and assure them she and Ama would do everything in their limited power to keep everyone informed. She encouraged the residents to band together with the same directive. To stop the sale going ahead.

In the previous weeks, Grayson had spent many evenings at Kamsi and Ama's flat relaying the background information he had gathered from Piers. For his troubles, they had made him drink a lot of *Kunu*, a thick milky-textured millet based drink that the sisters were fond of. He was not. Whilst it reminded them of the more pleasant times of their childhood. It reminded him of them force feeding him throughout his.

'It will help you grow big and strong.' They used to preach.

Joel would always finish his first. He loved it. Grayson would drink it, but did not like the taste. It did, however, make him feel cared for back then. That warmth resonated even more so now.

What Grayson had told them concerning the Estate had shocked them. They made a conscious decision, for now, to soften the message to the residents until they knew more facts.

Grayson learned that the understaffed and under-funded councils of London were keen to raise funds through the disposal of assets. With multi-family buildings and tower blocks, as found on the *Cranbrook Estate, Tower Hamlets Council* were keen to remove themselves from liability for the insufficient and unsafe living quarters. They did not have the money, nor expertise to bring the buildings up to standard, or even to a level which wouldn't carry the burden of fault, should the worst happen. As it did at *Grenfell*.

Where there is death and devastation, there are also

vultures. Private Equity firms were circling. Multi-billion pound organisations run out of their Mayfair offices, preyed upon situations of distress. And not only financial distress, environmental and social levers could be just as appealing, if not more so, because in forced sales, there lies the true exploitative value.

The value was ready to be worked, mined and extracted through asset management. The modern-day coal face. Without the blistered hands, black lungs or need for a canary. A case of buying the estate, modernising and 'bringing up to a standard' which would legally justify moving the rents to 'market levels', often three-times the current rate. In making these highly profitable changes, the social component of the housing would all but evaporate. Longstanding tenants forced to leave their homes, displaced from the very areas they were born and bred. Social cleansing glossed over in less controversial terms, such as gentrification.

Adhering to an expanding central London and the needs of the burgeoning white-collared middle class. More often than not, white was not just the colour of the collar. Ten years ago, these new inhabitants wouldn't have ventured too far off of the tube at Bethnal Green, but following the London Olympics, large swathes of the East End had experienced such a fate, their residents displaced, dispersed and with them the history, tradition and integrative nature of the East End. New developments often lacked soul and delivered only sanitised culture.

The reality was the *Grenfell* disaster had lowered values of council-run estates and increased the pressure on the local authorities to sell. Waiting for formal notification would be too late. Grayson had also learned that *Tower Hamlets Council* already had a buyer lined up, an American firm, the Black Spear Group.

Looking around the hall as Kamsi concluded her speech.

Shocked, the residents did not ask any follow-up questions. It would take a while to sink in. It also surprised Grayson just how quickly things were moving behind the scenes. A landlord that took years to address the smallest of maintenance issues, lining up the sale of the hundred-million-pound estate in a matter of months. To him, it illustrated how undervalued the *Cranbrook Estate* was in the eyes of the Council. And how aggressively eager private equity was to get their hands on it.

He was so proud of Kamsi. Her journey had not been easy. She had struggled to settle in London. She had found it tough to adapt to the damp weather, the rush and bustle of the high street had overwhelmed her. When Ama had first started at the hospital, Kamsi felt isolated and lost. She would retreat to bed the moment Ama left the flat. She had wished for a more simple life, as she had growing up in Kano. The appointment at the *Community Centre* inspired her to battle the depression head-on and make this little part of London her home.

He felt his frustration towards Joel increasing. Wanting to avoid a further awkward engagement with him, as the speech ended, Grayson gave Kamsi a congratulatory smile and slipped out of the hall.

11 BAD BEAT

Norton House, Cranbrook Estate, Bethnal Green, E2

6 December 2017

Large iron radiators that scalded to touch, and the wall-to-wall bodies, now charged with emotion. As he swung open the Community Centre doors, the heat rushed out and hit the frozen fog. Grayson zipped his jacket to his chin but was impervious to the cold, now smouldering at Joel's nonchalance. Seeing the bravery Kamsi displayed as she faced her fears made him even more angry that Joel had succumbed to his. Kamsi had leaned on Ama for support, yet Joel could not confide in him.

He crossed the uneven paving slabs to the gate and set off across the estate. Shards of glass and plastic crunched underfoot as the pathway fell into darkness. He scanned the buildings. Only a few of the windows housed illuminated curtains. The rest were lifeless. He looked back to the

Community Centre. The upper windows aglow, a beacon that had called for the residents to gather, bringing with them their light and warmth.

A solitary light caught his eye. He diverted across the grass towards it. Midway across he paused and stared up to the small single window. The room beyond he knew well, but it had been close to fifteen years since he occupied it. Fifteen years since he packed up what few items he possessed and began a fresh start. As he looked up to his old bedroom, he imagined his younger self peering out towards him. Towards the fog, towards darkness.

'A fresh start.' That is what Kamsi had called it as she greeted him with open arms as he pushed open the door. Busy at the kitchen sink, she wore an array of colours, yellow marigolds, a white tee-shirt rolled shoulder high, a vivid green headband and a violet apron. The brightest of all was the smile she wore.

For a six, almost seven-year-old Grayson, the small flat in Norton House would be a fresh start. It was the best thing in the world. It didn't matter that his new bedroom was tiny; it was warm, and painted blue, his favourite colour. Best of all was the view. If he laid on his bed and cranked his head skywards to the fifth floor of the opposing building, he could see Joel's window. Ok, it wasn't his bedroom; it was the lounge, but that didn't matter, they could still communicate by flashing the light on and off, like a secret code.

He would also see Ama and Kamsi every day. In fact, after school, he could see Kamsi whenever he wanted. She was always around, either at her flat or thirty-eight seconds away in the Community Centre. Thirty-eight seconds, it was the first thing he tested. He ran so quickly he may have lost count. He wanted to try it again and asked his dad to time him, but he told him no, and instead to take his bag and box up to his bedroom.

Grayson later learned that with his dad not working and spending pretty much all the dole money on drink, the repossession of their house on Old Ford Road had become inevitable. Kamsi had sprung into action and exhausted every favour she had ever earned to lobby the Cranbrook Tenants and Residents Association and push Niall's name to the top of the waiting list. She was instrumental in the effort to get them that flat. And give them that chance to rebuild their lives.

Although Grayson could spend more time with Joel and see Kamsi and Ama every day, it hadn't been the fresh start he hoped for. In fact, things got progressively worse. About six months later, the bank sold their repossessed house. The amount had exceeded what his Dad had owed them. So one early afternoon, as he recovered from the night before, his dad stumbled to the doorway and found a cheque for eight thousand pounds sitting in a pile of post. For most, it would have been a chance to reset, some stability and an opportunity to get back on-track, but for a man well passed tipping point, it sent him quicker on his downward trajectory of alcohol fuelled grief.

Grayson looked from the bedroom window across to the dark empty lounge and then down to the tidy front garden. He lasted a further seven years in that flat. After spending as much time as he could at school, playing with Joel at Ama and Kamsi's and in the community centre he would reluctantly retreat home. He would confine himself to his room, so as not to cross paths with his dad. He was always upset, drunk, or both. Never concerned if Grayson was home or not. At first the pain of the emotional abandonment manifested in crying fits. Unheard or unwanted, they never brought his dad running. Left to control his emotions he learnt to seek comfort in numbers and patterns, and to steady his breathing. He sat hours at a time reciting sequences of playing cards, forming elaborate stories to help him remember. He spent hours emotionally imprisoned in that room.

From time to time, when his father had left for the evening, he would sneak down to the kitchen. Initially he scavenged for food. Over the years taught himself to cook basics. Stealing items from various corner shops and supermarkets in the area. A tin of beans here, a loaf of bread there. For seven years it continued. It was just before his fourteenth birthday when Mr Patel from the corner shop had realised his inventory of *Clipper* lighters, *Marlboro Light* and *Benson* cigarettes was in deficit. The CCTV camera that pointed to the shop counter was a fake. He hadn't caught Grayson red-handed, but given the item specifics he put two and two together. With no hard-and-fast evidence, Mr Patel charged Niall for the missing items the next time he was in the shop stocking up on whisky.

Grayson had pleaded his innocence. Initially he denied all knowledge, but after a long confrontation he broke down and told his dad the truth. It had been Joel who had stole the items. Inpatient with their small profits, Joel had wanted to earn more money. Grayson confessed. He had been in the shop, but was unaware of the role he had taken until afterwards. Whilst Grayson had distracted Mr Patel pointing towards the top shelf chocolate boxes, Joel had pocketed the goods. Grayson had told his dad the full account, but he hadn't believed him. He got angrier and angrier the more Grayson tried to shift the blame to Joel.

Most of the argument Grayson had blocked from memory. Even now as he faced the very spot he stood that day, he struggled to piece together the sequence. He ran his finger over the scar below his eye and peered back up to the window. He pictured himself sat frozen on the floor, he daren't move. Loud voices in the lounge. Ama, Kamsi and his father's. Then the voices fell silent and there was a knock on the door. It was Kamsi.

'Grayson,' she said softly 'pack your clothes. We have decided you will stay with us for a while.'

He left that evening. That was the last time he was ever in that room. He moved the short distance to Ama and Kamsi's flat, to share an even smaller room with Joel.

By the time Grayson left that day, the front garden was overgrown with grass and weeds. Full of litter, that had never been picked up. The broken window effect. When a broken window, or littered garden, is taken as a sign of anti-social behaviour. Its existence further encouraged civil disorder. More and more people throwing litter into the garden. A perpetuating downward spiral of urban decay. And that is what father had been, broken. Since the moment his mother had past he had been stuck in his own downward spiral. A perpetual cycle eroding at every aspect of his life. The last thing Grayson knew, having defaulted on the rent and been kicked out of the Estate, he had ended up in supported housing somewhere nearby.

'Not even saying laters now brah?' Joel arrived at his side, his gym bag slung over his shoulder.

'Followed you out and been watchin' you standing here for ten minutes now. You're proper shook.'

Grayson remained silent, his stare fixed on the front door of the flat.

'Look, the guy's a prick. No point in being here beatin' yourself up on it.'

Grayson could sense the dark humour coming. He knew Joel too well and knew he couldn't stand the silence.

'Quit your whining, at least you have an old man. Even if he is a proper dickhead.'

Grayson couldn't maintain. He cracked a smile.

Fuck he infuriated him. Joel had this ability to break tension. A paper layer of charm over the cracks of deceit.

Perhaps this was the time to address the issue and talk about the casino, the money and come clean about the business. The fact that in just two days time he would go ahead with the game without him.

'Look, I know about...' he trailed off.

No. Now was not the time. He should leave it for now, give Joel space to train. To focus on the fight. That side of things was on-track. Pulling him up on the gambling now would force him into a corner and apply unnecessary pressure. After all, he had no more money to lose.

'Know what?' Joel said.

Grayson turned his face back towards the flat as he thought fast.

'I know...' a beat passed, 'I know you're worrying for Kamsi but she's got this. She was great in there tonight.'

'Of course Brah. She's family.' Joel's grin met Grayson's look.

Standing there facing the demons of his past, talking to the friend that saved him. He couldn't help but love this guy, but trust was broken.

'Back to it?' Grayson said, acknowledging the bag on Joel's shoulder.

'Everyday now. Twelve kilos to trim before weigh-in.' Joel gestured to the flat. 'Listen yeah. Don't worry yourself with all this shit. It's past times, yeah?'

Grayson agreed. Joel brought him in for a dap, before they set off in opposite directions across the Estate. The frustration had dissolved, replaced with regret.

12 BACK DOOR

9 December 2017

The *Acorn* pub stood on the corner of Queensbridge Road and Whiston Road, about a mile west of the *Cranbrook Estate*. A classic two-storey Victorian boozer, closed two years back. Set for redevelopment as part of the ongoing gentrification of this previously forgotten part of the East End. Out with the old, in with the new.

The dirty white stand-alone building, black boarded windows, shuttered front doors and hidden rear service entry made this the ideal location for a discreet card game. One that now attracted hefty buy-ins, but also the attention of a few of the faces from the neighbourhood. It was not a place where most would want to spend their Friday night.

Tonight, Grayson was going it alone. He didn't want to risk exposing Joel to the game or the money any longer. Joel was on the brink. His career too important and his addiction too strong. Seeing him in the casino the week before had made that clear. Enough was enough. He had finally had his breakthrough in the ring, landed the *Adidas Boxing* sponsorship and had fights arranged that gave him a pathway to a championship belt.

As Grayson ran through the final set-up and briefed James Johnson's crew, he tried to push aside the anxious feelings. Joel had always been there. From an early age they had had each other's backs. Grayson couldn't help but feel exposed. He had arranged security with a different crew, for the sole purpose that Joel would not hear about the game before they played it. He knew he would find out, eventually. The clock was ticking. That was a given, but he wanted to buy enough time to see his plan through. Chatter around the estates was bringing the game notoriety. Unwanted pressures accompanied with requests to play. Pressures that Joel specialised in resolving.

Buy-ins were ten thousand pounds for each player, over three tables of six players. The going rate for the venue and property security to turn a blind-eye was *a bag,* a thousand pounds. Same again for door security. A *monkey*, five hundred each for three trusted dealers and another *monkey* to stock the bar. With a seven percent rake, Grayson and Joel would clear close to ten thousand for their troubles. The clientele knew the game was straight. It was not without incident as players busted, but no one had ever tested Joel or the security crew. Grayson prayed tonight would not be a first.

Profits were not the only thing Grayson and Joel shared. Inseparable since the day they met, they had both developed an instinctive ability to read and gauge reactions, instantly deciphering outcomes. Through kid's games they had learned how to spot tells and calculate odds, but growing up on an East London estate, their skills shifted quickly toward interactions with the people and the shady characters around them. They had worked diligently to keep the gangs off their backs whilst they made a few quid.

Tonight, stakes were high. Not only had Grayson cut Joel from the game, but he had also decided to play. Excluding Joel meant that this would be the last game. He didn't want to run the business without him. Grayson decided that he would risk the guaranteed ten grand and sit at a table. He needed to maximise the exit profit for his plan to succeed.

With Joel running security, it wasn't uncommon for Grayson to play. His skill level was far superior to the players in the room. If he desired, he could take first place at a regular clip. However, he and Joel knew that taking their punters money to this extent would be bad for repeat business. It would also elevate the risk of disgruntled gangsters thinking the game was rigged and seeking retribution. Instead, he would normally sit to control the flow, move chips around and ensure that every now and again all players would get a taste of the winnings, go home with some cash. And, most importantly, an eagerness to return. Grayson would retreat out of chip leading positions and settle for third place, almost doubling their profits for the evening. It surprised them, that this strategy had gone unnoticed for so long.

The first of the players arrived. Without an entourage, they passed security. A light pat-down as they filed through the two-manned rear service door. Grayson's anxiety decreased as a recognisable form to the evening took shape. He still couldn't shake his friend's absence. He would be at the gym, or boxing club, training somewhere he assumed. He hoped. Maybe he would be with his aunties.

With competing levels of ego-led nonchalance as they took their seats, the players handed their buy-in cash to Lexi O'Shea, a dealer or a croupier as the casinos like to call them.

The cash typically came in two *gangster rolls*, bound wads each containing one hundred, fifty-pound notes.

Gary Merchant was the only player not to pay in *reddies*. It was his first time at the game and perhaps he didn't know the etiquette, but cash is cash. He had a somber look to his balding round face and beard of three-days growth. His big frame fitted into a brand new short sleeved shirt, red, white and blue checked. With embarrassment, he passed Lexi an envelope which contained a mixture of notes.

Lexi counted the money on the tables, before placing the wads in three separate holdalls. When the money was all in, the first place holdall would contain one hundred thousand pounds. The second place, fifty thousand pounds. And the third place holdall would hold seventeen thousand five-hundred pounds. After checking and counting the cash, Lexi would pass the holdalls to Grayson, who in full view of the players, would put them into a safe he had had installed on the far wall, after getting the keys to the venue.

Grayson had first met Lexi O'Shea at a blackjack table in the *Sportsman*, a small basement casino hidden behind Marble Arch tube station. Lexi was an attractive older lady, she carried confidence, wore impressive diamond jewellery and always maintained her blonde highlights and manicured nails. At the time, Lexi was using her third husband's name, Hannigan. Grayson had come to her aid, restraining the father of an F1 driver who was gambling with his son's money and luck had turned moments after her shift had started. As his chips dwindled, he hurled abuse her way, blaming her for the bad cards. Lexi, now in her late fifties, had seen it all before and took pleasure in winding-up men she thought to be arseholes, even if their kid was a hotshot. It was a habit of principal that had cost her a few jobs and a couple of husbands. It didn't take her long to get him to boiling-point, off his stall and screaming at her.

After the scuffle subsided and the table cleared, Grayson and Lexi had talked, realising they were born in the same neighbourhood. He played the table minimum whilst Lexi recanted stories of growing up in Bethnal Green in the eighties, in the aftermath of the Kray brothers. The evening ended with Lexi offering to deal Grayson and Joel's first poker game, which took place the following week in the basement of a disused bookie on Columbia Road. Nowadays that unit operated as a bourgeoisie residential estate agent. The bookies neon lights taken down, the facade restored to its Victorian glory and then coated in *Farrow & Ball* exterior emulsion. Mole's Breath the selected colour of the proprietor. Grey to anyone else walking by the E1 shop front. Lexi had been at every game since. As the game expanded to two and later three tables, she had organised the additional dealers. Grayson trusted her and importantly, so did the players.

Fifteen were in, seats drawn and allocated. On the whole, these were not men you wanted the company of. Mostly a charmless mix. Culturally lost Burberry-clad chavs, who built up their buy-in playing internet games for twenty hours a day and craved some real-life action. Or wide-boys in shiny suits spending commission from their last ten car sales. And low-life chancers, recycling cash from any number of schemes they run locally.

Grayson scrolled on his phone, mainly so he didn't have to talk or interact with anyone, but also to check the player list. With five minutes until the scheduled start, they were waiting on Steve Mason and Dave Squelch.

Steve Mason ran a window cleaning firm in the area. He was a reasonable, hard working type of guy, family man. He would attend the card game after a bumper month, or when he had booked a new client or two. Grayson didn't mind the man. Dave Squelch on the other hand was a horrid piece of work. When they first started the game, he was a low-level crook, chopping out stolen goods from the back of his transit, getting moved on by anyone with the smallest amount of clout. Over the years however, he had grown in stature and was now running a bunch of operations out of a small manner in Hackney Wick.

From the service door came raised voices. Grayson went to see what the commotion was. James Johnson was already there.

'He's not on the list boss.' He said moving his frame out of the way to reveal Lloyd Blake standing in the doorway.

Grayson had never seen an albino rat, but always associated a likeness. Scowling flaxen eyebrows, almost transparent against his pale face. A permanent expression of exacerbated anger. Tight cropped fire red hair, a large bottom lip, offset with his jaw. Both Grayson and Joel detested him. All the way through school and ever since, their paths had crossed on far too many occasions. Lloyd continually sought vengeance for the punch that led to the rewiring of his jaw.

'Tables are full. And no spectators.' Grayson said, taking a high road of formality, but then couldn't resist layering his rejection.

'So,' flicking his eyebrows into the distance, 'off-you-fuck!'

'Now now.' From the darkness emerged the stocky frame of Dave Squelch. No matter how cold, Squelch was never seen in a jacket or jumper. Always a polo shirt, always a size too small, fitted tight over his stomach and flabby pecks. Tonight's was grey and black with a white detail on the collar. As he stepped towards the light Grayson recognised the visible dents in his shaved head. His eyes close-set to the brow of his nose. He carried a indignant look on his face that was inherently intimidating as it portrayed a man at the end of the line, willing to undertake any act.

A condescending arm reached out to Grayson's shoulder. Fat fingers massaged their way up to his neck with an applied force that did not evoke a physical reaction from Grayson, but clearly indicated that what was about to be said should be strongly considered.

'Stevie Mason won't be joining us tonight. His wife has come down with the flu. Or she's washing her hair, or something.'

Not even attempting to make-up a plausible story. It was clear to Grayson that Squelch had waved off Steve Mason.

He released his grip and opened his palm as if to present Lloyd.

'Lloyd here will sit instead. Trust you don't have any problem?'

The imposing tone denoting it wasn't a question.

On the spot, Grayson ran through the situation. The three remaining seats in the room were on different tables, so they wouldn't be able to *chip dump*. Squelch and Lloyd Blake were up to something, but at that moment Grayson couldn't see the angle.

'He's never seen ten grand in his life.'

'Well today,' Squelch slowed as if to amplify the drama. 'It just so happens, he has it.'

Through gritted teeth, goaded and with immediate regret, Grayson said, 'look's like he's in then.'

13 SHOWDOWN

The Acorn, Queensbridge Road, Bethnal Green, E2

9 December 2017

Compared to what was to follow later that evening, the next three hours were uneventful, borderline boring. Exactly as Grayson had hoped for. Still, he couldn't help shake the feeling that without Joel alongside him, he was pushing his luck. He had disturbed the karma gods.

As the blinds increased, players busted out of the game. To Grayson's disbelief, Lloyd Blake was hanging on to the third place on his table. He was on the brink of elimination as Squelch took a three-way pot on his table, busting both of his last competitors.

Lexi called for the remaining six players to bring their chips and join the final table. She thanked her dealers and invited them to head home.

From Lloyd's table, Imran Kabir and Andrzej Topa arrived.

A sense of uniformity to their attire. Although previously unacquainted, both men of matching build, wore similar clothing. Loose fit black t-shirts drooped over their un-fit frames. Both also wore black *Adidas* caps. Kabir, a British-born Indian complimented his look with silver framed sunglasses. Although indoors, at night, in the middle of winter, the wearing of sunglasses was not out of place. Players taking every advantage possible to conceal their facial expressions. Kabir was an IT and computer science lecturer at *East London University*. A long time participant in the game. Of all the men involved in the evening, he posed the least threat to Grayson and was about the only one he could stomach.

Topa was Polish, originating from the small village of Raszyn, on the outskirts of Warsaw. He had made his way to London within weeks of the ascendancy of Poland to the EU. He had taken a job fitting high-end audio and visual equipment in swanky North London homes. He had shared a flat in Acton with five other Poles and would send most of his wages back home to his wife and family. Then one day a flatmate introduced him to internet gambling. In the years since the money transfers diminished to zero. Topa transitioned from the steady wage and moderated diet, to online poker as a full time occupation. He moved out of the shared flat and into a single ground floor bedsit on the *Arden Estate*, surviving on a diet of canned larger, *Uber Eats* and *Deliveroo*.

Already seated was Gary Marchant and Grayson. Dave Squelch strutted over to make up the six. He initially spun his chair through one-hundred and eighty degrees before squatting on to it and resting his elbows on the table's edge. Lexi shuffled the cards and began to deal.

It didn't take long for Lloyd Blake to expose himself. Grayson read him accurately. A small boy, trying to impress his boss. Dealt a *mid-pair*, Grayson assumed Jacks. For a novice, those Jacks looked strong. He pushed forward half his stack pre-flop, trying to conceal his Cheshire cat grin.

As Lexi dealt the flop, Grayson watched Blake. The read was 'nursery rhyme' easy.

Four (spades), his eyes grew wide. His pair looked good.
Eight (diamonds), his pale cheeks flushed with excitement.
King (clubs), his head dropped a fraction, as his eyes glazed over.

It was almost laughable to Grayson. Twinkle twinkle little star. Blake had tensed up, ready to take on the bluff, like a car passenger sliding to impact. His brakes had failed, he braced. Blake would go all-in, no matter what.

Sitting on the button, with King in-hand, Grayson was still unsure what Squelch and Blake were up to. He watched Squelch as Blake made the 'all-in' call. The utter look of disappointment that crossed Squelch's face amused him. Topa folded. Grayson was last to play, heads-up. He scoffed, called and flipped his cards on to the table. He neither acknowledged the win, or Blake, as he stood with nonchalance to pour himself a drink. Night-night, sleep well. As he returned to his chair he looked across to Blake.

'What are you still doing here? Why don't you scuttle off back to your mum's crack den?'

'Rich coming from you. Haven't seen your piss-head old man about and last I heard the maggots finished on your mum years ago.'

Grayson reared up from his chair in anger.

'Boys, boys,' Squelch chuckled. 'You're both scummy no goods, but we've got a game here. So Lloyd, you take a pew over there and pipe the fuck down.' Squelch directed Blake to an empty table.

Andrei Topa only lasted five more hands. Kabhir seemed to have a strong read on his play. He leant on him at every opportunity, whittling down his chips until he forced him to make some bold calls to survive. The last of which saw him go all-in on an open-ended straight draw and fail to pick-up the card he needed.

Grayson could sense Gary Marchant becoming impatient. He began to play hands with more frequency. Grayson was hoping for strong enough cards to take him on, but Squelch beat him to it, reading a weak bluff and matching his all-in bet.

Squelch didn't wait for Lexi to push the chips towards him. He stood, territorialising the table and formed stacks from the pot he had won. He dressed-down everyone left in the room. A one-man variety show, for a one-man audience of Lloyd Blake, now laid back in a chair, feet up on an empty table.

'It was a pleasure to play with you.'

The sarcasm directed at Gary Marchant, who had busted in fourth place. Jacket in-hand, he trudged to the door.

'I'll make a stack of your chips. Right here next to my drink.'

'Twat.' Gary fired back.

'Squirmy prick. Now do one.' He flicked his fingers to shoo him out the door.

Gary left the pub. Home no doubt. To get back online.

'Thanks for the cards darling.' Squelch said towards Lexi. 'Now be a good girl. And serve them up for me again.'

Lexi's restraint was visible. With Grayson well positioned in the game, she didn't want to cause him a problem or create a scene. She bit her lip. Squelch's time will come.

'See Son. This is how you deal with these little chancers.' Squelch gave out life lessons to Lloyd, who smugly lapped them up.

'And you.' He looked square at Grayson. 'It's about time you start your usual little party trick and start dumping chips.'

Until that point, Squelch had muttered and ranted, but it had all been white noise to Grayson. The last comment however jolted him to attention as an air of disappointment hit him. His previous schemes of profit apportionment had not gone unnoticed, as he thought they had. The oversight frustrated him. He now knew Squelch expected him to bail from the game. The control of the game wasn't his concern, it was that he knew Squelch would grow with hostility, especially as it become clear to him that Grayson planned to fight this one out to the end.

Now down to the final three players, Lexi shuffled the deck and dealt the cards. Grayson carried out a rough chip count. Each player had a similar stack; perhaps Squelch had more, but it was not significant. In theory, at this point the win could go to any player, but theory was far from reality. Grayson considered both Kabir and Squelch accomplished players. They gave off very few physical tells. For both players, exposure lay in their betting patterns. Kabir was conservative, he bided his time, his bet sizes and his position analysis was textbook. Squelch, on the other hand, was erratic, he had never studied strategy and often went on gut and emotion.

Grayson brought his hands up to his closed eyes. Pulled them down across his face as he feigned a moment's hesitancy. It was decision time. Not about the *call*. He knew he had Kabir covered. It was time to decide, once and for all, that he would push on. That he would pass third place and take a larger pot.

Kabir, Squelch, Lloyd and even Lexi seemed to think he was running through the odds. He was analysing, but not the cards. Step-by-step he reviewed every decision made since he chose not to intervene with Joel in the casino, his decision not to confront him at *Repton* and to press ahead for the first time in his life and run a scheme without his best friend. One-by-one, he re-litigated and green-ticked his judgements.

'Call.' Grayson announced.

He placed his cards face up on the table. The inevitable look of disappointment crossed Kabir's face.

Kabir bust, Lexi paused the game whilst Grayson stood to open the safe and retrieve the third place holdall. As he returned Kabir already had his jacket on. With a moderate level of dignity, he received the outstretched holdall and thanked Lexi for the evening as Johnson escorted him to the rear service door.

Grayson walked around the bar and poured himself a beer. With Kabir now gone, the tension in the room rose. As he retook his seat, he peered towards Johnson, who was returning to his stool by the door. Grayson reached into his pocket for his phone. He typed and sent a text message, before indicating to Lexi he was ready to continue.

'Down to two. Heads-up poker.' She announced.

Grayson and Squelch sat at opposite ends of the table. Each behind a fortress of chips. Their respective strongholds were of equal size. Both players could dig-in and ready their ramparts for war, but Grayson knew that was not Squelch's style. He was more blitzkrieg.

It was about the fifteenth round that was dealt when Squelch glanced to his chips. The nuanced tell was barely detectable, but the cagey behaviour after made it obvious. Squelch trying to goad Grayson to call his pre-flop raise. What Squelch hadn't accounted for was the cards Grayson held. Two Aces.

Grayson declared he was all-in and was quickly called by Squelch. Both players flipped the cards on their backs. Grayson so used to reading the reactions found himself analysing the rising anger of Squelch as Lexi flopped the first three cards, and with minimal delay the turn and river cards. Grayson's aces stood up.

He had won, but Squelch's anger had turned irate.

'Open the safe.' The instruction was calm and collected.

He needed no further persuasion as Squelch lifted a *Colt .45* handgun and pointed it towards Grayson's face.

'Now. Be a good lad and open the safe!'

Grayson shot a look to James Johnson, who stood inside the doorway to the pub. The read that he got from his reaction told him all he needed to know. He was in on it.

Now he had very limited options.

'Ok, ok.'

Grayson stood, turned and walked towards the safe. Squelch moved with him and maintained a two yard distance, the gun now fixed between Grayson's shoulder blades.

He paused at the safe door.

'Hurry up. You prick.' Lloyd piped up.

'Shut him up.' Grayson expelled in frustration.

He took a deep breath and reached to the safe. The dial cold and heavy in his hand. He turned in the code. Left 55, right 32. A stony silence. They could only hear the clicks of the combination dial as it ran through the numbers. Left 58 and right 67. A loud click signified the fence had dropped, releasing the bolt.

Grayson took one more deep breath, then turned the latch and swung open the door. Two holdalls sat in the safe. One hundred thousand in one bag and fifty thousand in the other.

'I don't suppose you fellas want to leave me the runner-up bag?'

Lloyd pushed in front of him, muttered an indecipherable rant, as he lifted out both bags.

'Right then.' Squelch announced.

'Thanks for the game. Especially you darling!'

'Low-life prick!.' Lexi snarled back at him.

'Cheers for the heads-up James.'

Grayson could only admire Squelch's brashness. With no hesitation he sold out the guy who brought him the idea. I guess that was his problem now. A small piece of consolation. And no wonder he had Lloyd play. It gave him more chances of being in the room at the business end of proceedings.

God only knows how they would have handled it if both Squelch and Lloyd had busted earlier. Would they have done this with others in the room? Would they have done this if it were someone else's winnings they were stealing?

With that, Squelch left the pub, Lloyd in tow. Grayson didn't bother to watch James Johnson and his men slink off into the darkness.

'What a bunch of assholes.' Lexi said.

'I know a few lads who could…'

Grayson cut her off. He knew where she was taking it.

'Lexi. Thanks, but this doesn't concern you. It'll be Ok. Why don't you head off home?'

'Are you sure?'

'It's fine. I'll close up here. I doubt there will be a next time, but I'll see you about, yeah.'

She placed a delicate hand of consolation on his shoulder.

'Ok then, if you're sure. Take care.'

With that, she swung her handbag up over her elegant beige trench coat and walked out, leaving Grayson alone.

He walked over to the bar and poured himself a large measure of whisky. Having had a gun pointed at his head for five minutes, he would have drunk whatever was on offer. It went down in one.

Grayson refilled the glass and sat still at the bar for two minutes as he ran through the evening's events. One-by-one he worked his way through the movements of the players. He wanted to make sure the only group involved comprised of Squelch, Lloyd, Johnson and his crew.

Only them, he concluded.

He reached into his pocket, retrieving his phone, wrote and sent a text.

'As expected. Meet you at NT's. I need a drink.'

Grayson stood and walked over to the safe. Opening the door, he peered inside.

Empty darkness.

He reached to the back and pulled on a latch. A false door to the rear opened. As he looked through the dusty hallway the other side, he released a gentle chuckle.

He shut the safe door, drank his whisky and was sure to turn off the lights and lock up on his way out.

14 HIGH STAKES

NT's Bar, Westgate Street, Bethnal Green, E2

9 December 2017

With a brief dap, Grayson passed by security as he entered NT's bar over on Westgate Street. The adrenaline was pumping as he bound up the four flights of stairs to the rooftop bar, one of his favourite hangouts in the East End. Casual dress, great drinks, unpretentious clients and good vibes.

As Grayson entered the room he spotted Piers in the far corner, wearing a blue turtle neck jumper and occupying some rustic leather sofas, a table full of cocktails and two bottles of *Bollinger* on ice. The dance floor was full. As if to signify his entrance the DJ was lifting the energy, smooth jazz beats giving way to vibed-out garage classics.

Piers stood, arms stretched to greet Grayson.

'Here is the man of the hour!'

Clearly he had started the celebration early. As he brought him in for a bear-hug. Grayson, still wired, was keen to confirm a few final details and wasted no time with pleasantries.

'Tell nobody about what went on tonight. Got it?'

'Got it. I'm just glad to have been of service. I was starting to feel guilty for taking your money old boy, to do, well, bugger all.'

'Just be grateful you weren't inside.'

Grayson had never expected to need Piers, or to use the safe's false door. He had devised the backup plan a couple of years earlier when the game expanded and stakes had increased. Joel had expressed concern that the makeup of their clientele was becoming more distasteful and he was uncomfortable bringing in anything more than pepper spray.

He was right. Joel had seen it coming. Highly intuitive, knowing when others would strike. That is what differentiated him from most. It would only be a matter of time before Joel found out that the game had gone ahead. He hoped he would have time to tell him first. Be able to sit him down and explain his reasoning for going behind his back. He hoped that his fifty-percent share of the money would go a long way to softening the blow.

'Drop-off went smoothly, I assume?' Grayson was never comfortable with assumptions.

Piers confirmed that after receiving the instructions by text message, he emerged from the shadows on Winston Road. He snuck into the pub through the side door. Opened the back of the safe and swapped out the holdalls. Then jumped into a taxi and deposited the cash in a deposit box at *Sharps Pixley*, at 54 St James's Street. Grayson enjoyed the irony of selecting a location two doors down from the casino.

Grateful for the detailed recap, Grayson reached for the *Bollinger*. As he popped the cork, his intensity dispersed.

By the fourth glass of Champagne, Grayson had settled into one of the large leather chairs, almost oblivious to the bustling dance floor next to him. As the adrenaline subsided, he began to review the evening.

He   smirked as he visualised the scenes at Squelch's industrial unit, not too far away in Hackney Wick. He imagined Blake and Squelch inspecting the contents of the holdalls, hearing their voices as they unveiled the surprise.

'What the fuck is this?' Squelch said.

'What's what?' Blake responds.

'What. The fuck! Is this?'

He pictured Blake standing there watching Squelch rabidly flipping through the wads of money in the holdalls, tossing them in every direction around the unit in disgust.

Blake picking up a wad to inspect the contents, finding it front and backed with a real fifty-pound note, but filled with bad imitation bills. Squelch's pace of examination quickening. And after turning both holdalls upside down and emptying the contents, he would pause, look up at Blake and with that snarl on his face scream.

'Get out there and find him! Find that fucking prick!'

Sheepishly Blake would put on his jacket and leave the unit. The freezing cold temperature and heavy rain would come as a relative relief to leaving the crazed man behind, armed with a *Colt .45* and a hundred and fifty thousand reasons to use it.

As the scene in his head concluded, he surmised in poker, as in life, you have to prepare for the downside and give yourself a chance to recognise a bluff. From the moment he excluded Joel from the game, he had assumed the worst and had planned accordingly.

Squelch turning up with Lloyd Blake at his side was

certainly a surprise. He knew they was up to something from the moment they arrived, but until the gun was drawn he did not know what. Not sure if it was a bluff, but when Squelch pointed it to his head, he hadn't wished to find out.

Grayson enjoyed his drink with a clean conscious. If Squelch, or anyone else had won the game straight-up he would've instructed Piers to leave the money in the safe and no-one would have been the wiser. He was glad that when someone attempted to cheat him, he had the backup plan in place.

A wide smile crossed his face. He now had the money to replace Joel's loss. A deed for his friend? Or relief from his own guilt? Either way, replacing the money would help Joel face-up to his problem and perhaps even come clean to his aunties and seek help. He was sure of it. And with Squelch 'forfeiting' his second place, there was a little extra, a foundation to move forward and build for the future. Perhaps allow Joel to put gambling and scheming behind him for good and focus on his boxing career.

He wished his friend could be with him in NT's to celebrate. Tomorrow he would resolve their issues. As for tonight, he concluded, he may as well enjoy it. He poured the remaining contents of a bottle into his glass and signalled to the waiter to send over another two.

As the waiter placed the new bottles in the ice bucket, Piers returned from the dance floor grinning ear-to-ear as he squeezed around the edge of the sofa.

'All right champ?' He laughed, acknowledging the refreshed bottles.

'This is Tessa,' He stepped round the low level table with two girls following, smiling at the seated Grayson. 'And this. This is Sofia.'

'They are visiting from Miami and are wondering why the English don't dance. As a gentlemen, I felt obliged for Queen and Country to show them my moves.'

Grayson stood to greet the girls, aware that his typical anxiety was absent. A moments thought of Estella took him to the pub, sat across from her as she told him it was over.

'Grayson.' Piers shouted over the music.

As his attention jolted back, Tessa used his outstretch hand as a lever to lean across the small table and kiss his cheek. Delightfully off-season surf blond hair. She wore a loose-fit maroon jumper, draped from her shoulder, playfully matched with a biege checked skirt and knee-high socks. Her sun kissed skin glistened in the light that spiralled off of the dance floor.

As Piers poured and passed out drinks, Sofia met Grayson with a wide smile. She had a latin complexion, with long brown hair, loose-curled around large hooped earrings. She wore a white tank top, beautifully simple against her olive skin and low-waist ripped jeans and heels that brought her a little closer to Grayson's height. No sooner had Piers raised a toast to the night, 'adventures had and to be had', the girls dragged Grayson and Piers on to the dance floor.

They reached the bottom of the stairs and looked out from the doorway through a torrential downpour. A taxi light shone from under the railway bridge twenty yards away. The four of them set off in unison to the dry protection of the bridge, the girls shrieking and giggling as they ran. The driver gave them a wry smile as they swung open the door and piled into the back.

'Evening. Where to?'

'Soho. Wardour Street.' Piers called out, as he jumped in.

The taxi reached the end of the road and indicated to turn right on to Mare Street. As they sat waiting for the green light, Grayson wiped the misted window and watched as the rain crashed down. Street lamps, shop signs and traffic lights blurred in a multicolour fog.

On the far side of the road, through the rain dashed window, he could make out the figure of a larger lady running towards a night bus, lugging several bags. The bags looked heavy and her footing treacherous on the broken pavement and pooling rain water. As she approached the bus stop, she dropped the bags as she waived and gestured to the driver in vain. The bus pulled away without her. His wing mirror no doubt misted over, the heavy rain drowning out any calls to wait.

As the taxi made the turn, the lady came into focus. Grayson stared in disbelief. He took a moment to absorb the shock and process the information, realising that the lady on the street was Kamsi. How much had he had to drink? Was he seeing things? No, he assured himself. It was definitely her. She was wearing a thick jacket and scarf he recognised.

He wiped the window again and looked through. She was bending to pick up no less than four bulky weaved bags now strewn on the street side as the rain continued to pour.

Instinctively, he called out to the driver.

'Can we stop mate?'

There was no response.

'Mate! Can we stop?'

Again nothing.

It took Grayson a second to realise that someone, most likely Piers, had turned off the taxi intercom. The button was out of his reach.

As he turned to slide the partitioning glass, the taxi sped up. With the momentum Piers dove off of his fold-back chair, landing between the giggling girls on the back seat.

Grayson, distracted by the sudden movement, struggled to slide open the glass behind his shoulder. As he twisted to open it and call to the driver, he began to question what he had seen.

Was it definitely her? Come on, you have seen her every week since you were six. You know it was. Maybe she wasn't going to the estate? There is no way she was heading anywhere else. How far is it? It's only a mile, maybe a fifteen-minute walk. It would have only been a five-minute diversion in the taxi in which he sat. It's soaking and freezing out there! Was there room? Of course there was. It is a Hackney Carriage. It has five seats.

The answers had come all too easy, yet he hesitated. Paralysed to decide.

As the taxi gathered speed, Grayson looked beyond Piers and the girls. Through the rain covered back window, the outline of Kamsi grew distant. He could just about make her out, as she struggled to pick up the bags, leave the bus stop and begin a wet walk back to the estate.

Guilt riddled reflection set in. He should stop the taxi, turn around and pick her up.

Sofia's soft hand touched his. Across the taxi, Tessa had a leg on Piers' lap, the two passionately kissing. Sofia's hand moved playfully up his arm as she slid up onto his outstretched knee, locking her arms behind his neck and staring into his eyes. A soft smile broke his intense gaze as she leaned in to kiss him.

15   HURT

Open. Shut.

Open. Shut.

Open.

Shut.

Frozen, thumb and forefinger primed to open the mirrored cabinet door once again.

The click startled his conscience. A beat passed as he realised the focus of his stare was his focused reflection.

How long had he been stood there?

Grayson had gone to the bathroom to retrieve Aspirin, Alka Seltzer, Ibuprofen, frankly anything that might offer relief from his piercing headache, but when had that been? A minute ago? Ten? Twenty?

He brushed off the thought, opened the cabinet once more,

retrieved a small pack of pills and threw some to the back of his throat.

Frozen pipes creaked as he opened the tap and cupped icy water to his mouth, but it wasn't enough. Needing immediate relief, he dropped his head to meet the flow. The water washed over his face as he drank until he gasped for air.

As he raised his head to the mirror, water escaped his gaped mouth and fell to the sink. Eyes bloodshot, the splayed red a stark contrast to the piercing blue.

His preoccupation was with the girl that lay in his bed and his wishing she wasn't there. No longer fuelled by alcohol and adrenaline, the thought of the morning interaction brought a gut-wrenching anxiety. Looking deep into the reflection of the black rings beneath his eyes, he questioned his actions.

A combination of anger and guilt swelled as his thoughts turned to Estella. Even though she had finished things between them, his behaviour didn't feel appropriate. It was out of character. He didn't believe they were finished, but he knew he had to do better by her and this was about the worst possible start.

Balance jittery, he made his way back to the bedroom. The white walls greyed by the morning gloom, hungover from the relentless downpour the night before.

The girl lay content. Dishevelled brown hair sprawled across the pillow. Hip-to-toe tanned skin exposed from the ruffled white duvet. A moment of admiration brought him ten times the guilt.

Sat on the edge of the bed. His pale skin taut, he shivered as his head continued to spin. He needed to lie down. He did so, but with apprehension as he pulled the duvet to cover him. The warmth she radiated came as a mild relief.

She stirred awake, a half smile broke full with gentle laughter. Refusing to open her eyes, she reached out and found his defined torso. She ran her fingers up to his stubbled jawline, across his cheek, pausing at the scar below his eye. Her forefinger continued to caress his face before coming to rest on his lower lip. She guided her head towards his, and open her eyes to his as she delivered a short, animated kiss.

She bound to her feet and in an effortless motion, recovered her torn jeans from the floor and slipped into them. He could not help but admire her form as she clasped her simple black bra against her olive skin beneath her breasts. Then delicately slid the bra round her body before lifting a strap to her shoulder. Her tact graceful, she paused and offered him a soft smile of recognition, before attending to the second strap.

She planted one knee on the bed at his waist and leaned over him, letting her long brown hair fall encapsulating an intimate space between their faces. Her scent sweet but foreign to him. He lay still and unsure.

'Amazing night,' she whispered with a subtle American accent, 'we should do this again sometime,' and leaned in with a soft kiss.

In a panic Grayson moved to lift her away, but paused with awkward reservation and instead ran his hands up her arms. She reached up to the side table for her mobile phone and playfully rested her cleavage to his face.

'Shit,' she laughed, 'I've got to run! We go to Paris this morning.' Her eyes wide with excitement. Although still dusty, he recalled their conversation from the night before. Their voices had barely carried above the thumping music as they skirted from the table to the dance floor. She and a friend were visiting from Florida. A whistle-stop tour of three European cities and their Christmas markets had them booked on the *Eurostar* that morning.

An ease come to him as he realised she was leaving.

She bounced up, slipped into her loose fitting white tank

top and recovered her long navy jacket from the back of a chair.

'Sleep well,' she jested as she slid on her high heels and headed to the door.

He mustered a forced smile as she left.

The room fell silent.

A lot to confront. Not least was Squelch, who no doubt by now had gone to count the money in the stolen holdalls and found the fake notes. Grayson had no doubt that retribution would be on the cards. In reacting to the situation and utilising the false safe door, he hadn't had time to fully consider the ramifications of pissing off a local *face*. Over the years the stature of Squelch had increased and with it his reputation for violence. Grayson would have to come up with a plan, and sharpish.

So often he had avoided such situations. More often than not it was Joel to thank for that, but having cut him out of the game, he couldn't exactly go crying to him now. No, he concluded, he would have to resolve this one alone. He knew his friend would find out soon, and when he did, he would be pissed. He liked to think he would be able to control Joel's reaction and anger, but he knew deep down he couldn't.

Determination quickly faded. Depleted, he stared up at the ceiling and considered just how alone he was. He would turn to Estella, but she had made it clear she didn't want to play games anymore. She had drawn a line under their relationship and cast him off.

As he began with the self pity, the source of his anxiety struck him. Kamsi. He replayed the moment over and over. The moment he drove past in the taxi. He had seen the bus drive by leaving her exposed to the horrific downpour and freezing winter temperatures. Everything she had ever done for him and yet he was too caught up in his own world to lend her a hand, stop the taxi and pick her up.

He would have a gangster breathing down his neck. He had betrayed his best friend. The girl he loved had left. Yet it was leaving Kamsi there in the cold that made him feel most like shit. Too exhausted to face the torrent of thoughts any longer, he shut his eyes and slipped into a deep slumber.

♠

He woke with a start.

At the foot of the bed towered a jet black silhouette.

PART II

16 COLD CALL

With each day, the number of flowers and hand written tributes grew. Five days later they now lined the entire length of the Community Centre fence. Sentiment, sympathy and colour, laid against a desolate backdrop of a building that had lost its spirit and soul. Word of Kamsi's death travelled through the Estate and around the wider Nigerian and minority communities. Locally, Kamsi touched the lives of many. Those further afield that didn't know her had warmed to the story of such a selfless and kind community leader, feeling compelled to make a dedication in her honour.

Grayson and Joel split their visits so Ama was not alone in the flat for too long. They worked a timetable around Joel's training. It was about 3pm as Grayson made his way to the Estate. The daylight had diminished, relentless grey clouds covered the sky.

As he walked past the laid tributes towards Ama's block he couldn't help but replay the call over and over. It wasn't the words that haunted him; it was the chilling noise. The likes of which he had only heard once before. The pain and fear his father released as his mother closed her eyes for the last time. On that day, it was Ama who had caught him. She wept as she held him tight. Every day since, she had been there for him. He was determined to return the love and support, now that she faced the most desperate moments.

Flowers also lined the damp concrete steps and ramped walkway to the tower block. By the main door, someone had placed a teddy bear alongside a collage. Pink and red materials mounted on a heart-shaped cardboard cutout. Grayson picked up the tributes to take inside to Ama, but hesitated and respectfully replaced them. Ama should see them in-place. As well as the hundreds that lined the Community Centre.

As the lift doors opened, he locked eyes with his reflection in the cracked, graffiti-ridden mirror. Guilt tormented every pure feeling of loss and remorse. He could not shake it. He was to blame for Kamsi's death. It would have been the smallest and easiest of gestures to turn the taxi back. She would have not needed to walk in the freezing cold wet weather back to the Estate. If he did so, she would still be here and there would not be a police investigation.

The Family Liaison Officer assigned to the case was Constable Kerry Pearson. A short blond girl, with clammy-red cheeks that gave her sympathetic gestures real sincerity. She had visited Ama a few hours after Kamsi had been killed, and had answered the door to Grayson who had rushed over immediately upon receiving Ama's call.

After Grayson's arrival and ensuring Ama was seated comfortably, she told them it was her first FLO designation.

'I completed the training just two weeks ago.' She said.

Her manner suggested she was yet to be burdened by the incalculable cases of tragedy and grief she would no doubt experience in her career.

'Our understanding thus far is that shortly before 1 am on Saturday morning, Miss Olakunbi was struck by a taxi on Bishops Way. Initial indications are that the blow had been to her upper body and the trauma to the head would have been instantly fatal.'

She peered up to the watchful eye of her superior officer, Detective Sergeant Margaret Cullen, before adding.

'We have opened a case file, investigating the full circumstances of the incident and will follow up at regular intervals.'

Ama was clearly upset, but as she took in Pearson's words she seemed reassured. She had witnessed a lot of suffering in her job at the hospital. Many times in her life as a nurse, explaining the next steps to those grieving and in shock had been a task that she had to undertake. She knew the steps, but it made it no less painful.

Ama initially requested to visit the site. She got as far as the door, but at the last moment recanted, held back the tears as she removed her coat, hat and gloves before she escaped in to the privacy of the kitchen.

Grayson sat with the police officers in the lounge, giving her space to grieve. She was a proud lady, doing everything in her power to keep it together in front of the officers, no matter how natural it would have been to break down. She returned from the kitchen with a pot of tea and a brave smile.

Ama had not left the flat since receiving the news. Each time Grayson arrived, as he placed his key in the lock, she had met him at the door. Following a hug, she then moved around the flat, endlessly cleaning and dusting every inch over and over. Anything to distract her from Kamsi's absence.

Inevitably, she would breakdown in tears. A different trigger each day.

It was agony for Grayson to watch with no way to help. Exhausted she would collapse on the sofa, drained of emotion. She would every now and again mention her sister, although never in the past tense.

This afternoon, however, as Grayson opened the door to the flat, Ama didn't meet him. The lounge sat dark. The gloomy grey covered sky relinquished barely enough light for Grayson to navigate to the kitchen. There he found Ama sat at the table, head in her hands, her shoulders quivered as she cried uncontrollably.

'Ams. Ams, what is it?' Grayson drew a chair close and embraced her with an arm across her shoulders. 'Ams, Ama. Look at me'. He encouraged her to look up. She slowly obliged, beginning to compose herself as she raised her head.

'They're closing the case.' She forced out as she searched Grayson's eyes for comprehension.

'They're closing the case.' She repeated.

Grayson locked eyes as he processed what she was saying.

'I don't know what to do?' She said, as her head fell and returned to her tear soaked hands.

As he took in the information, Grayson could see that what had brought on this emotional state wasn't the actual closing of the case. No, the thought of having to receive her sister's body and put her to rest haunted Ama. No longer a state of absence, but a state of permanence.

Pearson had called Ama earlier that morning to let her know she was on her way to see her and that the case would now be closed. The determination that Kamsi's death was accidental. They diagnosed the cause of death as a cerebral contusion. The Road Policing Senior Investigating Officer, referred to as the RP SIO, under advisory of the Collision Investigator determined that all analysis from the scene pointed towards an accident. The driver provided a clean breathalyser result and a detailed statement. They also noted that evidence illustrated that the vehicle was driving within the speed limit.

Ama's mobile rang. She tried her best to compose herself as she answered it.

'Yes. Ok. Please.'

Pearson and Cullen had arrived at the main door and made their way up. Grayson turned the lounge lights on and opened the door for them.

After ensuring Grayson would make a pot of tea and give her the opportunity to speak one-on-one with Ama, Pearson sat Ama down on the sofa and perched on the side chair. She faced Ama clasping her hand in hers as she spoke clearly and directly to her, maintaining eye contact throughout as she described the steps the Investigating Officers had taken.

They had placed a Notice of No Further Action in the file. The case was to be closed. The Collision Investigator in liaison with the coroner determined that Kamsi had slipped. Bruising around her left ankle suggesting she had rolled it on the curb, propelling her into the road as a taxi struck her.

A look of shock took hold of Ama.

'Why was she there?' The questions came in panic. 'How can it be?'

'We don't know why, but it was an accident. We know Kamsi fell...' Pearson could no longer mask her compassion behind the textbook dialogue she delivered to Ama.

A firm hand on her shoulder stopped her mid-sentence. Margaret Cullen stepped in and drew Ama's attention from Pearson.

'Unfortunately, the reasons for Miss Olakunbi being on Bishops Way, at that time and in that weather, are outside the scope of the investigation undertaken. Especially considering clear evidence that there was no fowl-play involved in her death.'

'What evidence?' Grayson questioned from the kitchen doorway.

'We are not at liberty to disclose the content of our inquiry, nor identify the evidence used in coming to the determination.' The delivery was textbook. It left no room for him to question further, but the statement didn't sit well with him. Clear evidence. He had seen first hand how bad the weather was that night. He was sure of one thing; nothing was clear.

'The coroner will be able to release the body of Miss Olakunbi in a couple of days. So you will be able to finalise funeral arrangements.' Cullen said, as she placed a set of documents on the side table and prompted for Ama to sign a receipt.

As Pearson and Cullen departed, the flat fell cold and horrifically quiet. Grayson stuttered in anguish as he attempted to break the silence. As he and Ama sat in the lounge, no matter how hard he tried, he couldn't come up with any words. Ama had undergone terrible traumas earlier in her life. In a will to cope, she had developed a strength to help others. She had devoted her life to be there, in their moment of need. Although devastated himself, Grayson knew that this would now be Ama's toughest test, and the path of grief had only just begun. He knew all too well from the loss of his mother, there was no such thing as a full recovery.

In his heart, he hoped that Ama would soon return to work at the hospital. It would be a small but meaningful distraction from the torture she was putting herself through stuck in the flat. It would be the best way for her to deal with tragedy. She would focus her energy, as she had done when she fled Nigeria and started a life in London's East End.

With heavy exhaustion, Ama slumped on the sofa. The emotions had taken their toll, giving way to a drained slumber. Grayson lifted the *Hausa, a* patterned throw from behind the sofa, and laid it across her. He left a glass of water on the table under the glow of the reading lamp and turned off the main light as he quietly closed the flat door.

Exhausted, but he knew he would not sleep. Questions and emotions pulsed through his mind. A piercing migraine and aching shoulders. His desolation towards Kamsi's death felt fraudulent under the weight of guilt. He left her in the cold wet rain to fend for herself moments before her death. If he had done the honourable thing and directed the taxi to pick her up, she wouldn't be dead and Ama would not be suffering.

As he walked to Bethnal Green tube station, his phone rang. With reluctance he took it from his pocket. He didn't recognise the number.

'Hello.'

He did recognise the voice.

'Listen, you little prick! Unless you want to end up like her, you better make good on the money you stole from me.'

17 CHECK

COUPETTE, 423 BETHNAL GREEN ROAD, E2

15 DECEMBER 2017

At the darkest end of the bar, Grayson sat and stared motionless at the double measure of whisky sitting on the table in front of him. The glass carried weight. Too much to lift for now. So he sat, lost in regret, playing the moments from that night over and over. Trying to grasp to the moment he decided not to turn around for Kamsi. As if, if he concentrated hard enough, he could go back and change the outcome.

A simple choice, to do the right thing and he chose wrong. The decision would haunt him. The call he had made was inexcusable. In an instant, he had discarded every principle he thought he held and he would now have to live with the consequences.

There were forces of occurrence he couldn't understand.

The same forces that urged him to sit there alone in the bar, drinking to ease the pain. A son, a shadow of his father. Unable to cope with grief. Set on a course to destroy his resentful life one measure at a time.

The glass of amber liquid sat on the table. A symbol of resignation. One thing stopped him for reaching for it. A sickening sense of anger. He replayed the words over and over.

'Unless you want to end up like her, you better make good on the money you stole from me.'

Moments before receiving the unnerving call from Dave Squelch, he had been informed that Kamsi's death was an accident. From the moment the Police told him, it didn't sit right. It was too coincidental, there were too many unanswered questions. Squelch's words confirmed that. Anger now exceeded the grief. It exceeded the remorse and exceeded the guilt.

'Thought I would find you here.' Joel emerged and stood over him. 'You know it hurts me when you drink alone.'

Grayson raised his head and responded before making eye contact.

'It hurts me too, but you have a fight in three weeks. The last thing I want,' he paused. 'The last thing Kamsi would want, is you throwing away your shot, sitting here drinking with me.'

In a show of defiance, Joel reached to the glass on the table and drank it in one, before turning to the bar and ordering two more.

'It doesn't stack up.' Grayson muttered to himself

'What doesn't? Joel asked.

Grayson wanted to come clean and tell Joel he had arranged the game without him. That he had seen Kamsi that night and could have picked her up. He wanted to tell him about Squelch's phone call. He craved the guilt release-valve, no matter the consequences. But like Joel not telling him about the losses at the casino, he stayed quiet. It was eating him up.

Joel offered a nod of thanks to the barman as two double measures arrived.

Attention turned back to Grayson, it took only a moments' silent attention to extract an explanation.

'They're closing the case.'

'What do you mean closing the case?'

'Exactly that. They have carried out all the investigations they plan to. And have concluded it was an accident. That she fell.'

'The driver?'

'Sober. Family man apparently. No record. No points on his licence and his first ever accident.' Grayson relayed what little information he had extracted from the FLO officer, out of the earshot of her senior colleague.

'And why was she there? Why was she out so late?'

'They don't know. "Outside the scope of their enquiry."' Grayson made it clear that he was quoting the officers.

'More like they can't be bothered to investigate the death of a black woman in the East End.' Joel expelled in frustration.

'There's that,' Grayson concluded, 'but also they seem far too convinced it was an accident.'

'You think otherwise?'

'She can't of fell! You don't just fall out into the road.' Of that, Grayson was sure. The whisky burned, as he delivered it to the back of his throat in a sharp aggressive pour.

'I know, but what can we do about it?'

Grayson was convinced that it was more than just an accident. Squelch's phone call, the atmosphere that night, or the fact that she was out so uncharacteristically late, and in such harsh conditions. There had to be a reason and that reason was related to her death. He was sure of it.

'What I will do about it, is find out why she was there. And why she was out so late.'

He reached out to beat Joel to his glass. Locked eyes with him in a show of determination.

'And what you will do, is win your fight.'

'We can't bring her back. There will be plenty of time afterwards for answers. And any retribution. You get the job done. You have come too far. She wouldn't want you to throw it away now.'

With a slow and reluctant nod of agreement, Joel comprehended the levity with which Grayson made the assertion. He took the drink from Grayson's hand.

'If I'm working, you're working too.' He said as he tipped the contents into the sink on the other side of the bar, stood and shoved Grayson's jacket to his chest.

As they stepped out of the bar on to the street, the wall of cold air hit them, catching them both short of breath. Joel's gym gear far less suited to now freezing temperatures. He lifted his hood over his black woollen hat.

'You look like you have a plan.'

'Yeah, of sorts. I know where to start.' Grayson said with a determined confidence.

'Bell me when you have news.' Joel said as he clasped Grayson's hand and arm and brought him in for a dap.

They parted in opposite directions.

18 CHASE

Piccolo Bar, 7 Gresham Street, London, EC2

18 December 2017

The mid-town location of *Piccolo Bar* on Gresham Street is a regular morning meeting spot for Black Cab drivers. An optimum location with quick access to and from the City and the West End. From the crack of dawn, Cabbies are drawn to the warm bacon rolls, strong Italian coffee and British 'Builders' tea. The large chilled glass counter also paid homage to Anglo-Italian unity with traditional British cakes appetisingly set out next to warm Italian breads and sandwich fillings. The drivers trickle in throughout the morning, but it is from ten until twelve when you will find most gathering for a post-rush hour break. An opportunity to discuss the football results, moan about the misses, or curse *Uber*, the pricing, the driving skills and the lack of *knowledge* the drivers possess.

It had taken Grayson less than half-an-hour to get this information. As well as the *Arches Cafe*, the cavernous railway arches on Three Colts Lane in Bethnal Green host a dozen car mechanics, which carry out repairs on most of the *Hackney Carriage* fleet of London.

The owner of the first garage was happy to divulge to Grayson a shortlist of five main Cabbie hangouts, once he had sussed out he was a local. By the third garage, they had given him details of the *Piccolo Bar*. Where, before the incident, he could find Mike Greenwood five or six days a week, placing his order of a fried egg and sausage sandwich with brown sauce. Accompanied by a milky tea with three sugars.

Having armed himself with a copy of the *Sun* newspaper in an attempt to fit in, Grayson now sat in the *Piccolo Cafe*. He looked round at the wooden chairs and Italian marble table tops that gave the place a pleasant uniformity. No doubt the owner got a job-lot for his four cafes, from a friend or relative in Verona. Grayson's intentions had been to sit with stealth and listen in to the conversations and mutterings surrounding the incident that had killed Kamsi a week earlier.

He wanted to build a picture of Mike Greenwood, outside of that which he had got online. A family man in his late fifties. Born, bread and living in Wanstead. Married for thirty-two years to his school sweetheart Kim. Two daughters, Kelly and Abigail, both in their late-teens, both with 'public' *Facebook* and *Instagram* accounts, a key source of Grayson's initial information gathering. An array of photos, documenting their lives and family events. Most recently Kelly's nineteenth birthday, Abigail's new *Ford Fiesta*, a present from dad for being accepted to *Birmingham University*, Mike and Kim's Pearl anniversary party. And most interestingly, photos of their new front garden showing both the house number and the street sign on the corner.

On the face-of-it Mike Greenwood seemed like a hard-working, upstanding bloke. A member of the *Worshipful Company of Hackney Carriage Drivers* for twenty-two years. After renting a Cab for the first twenty years of his career, his daughters were incredibly proud that in early 2015 he bought a brand new TX4 model outright. They had posted many photos of him and the family standing alongside the vehicle, Prosecco in hand. Finally, a proper '*Musher*' they declared. The comments below stated that he had reluctantly accepted a small *livery* on a two-year contract from *Vodaphone* to raise the final money needed. Abigail had joked that it was that, or they would have to cancel the family holiday to Tenerife. Further comments reported that he loved the Cab, but couldn't wait to remove the bright red signage as soon as possible. Although affectionally referred to as the 'Little Red Bus', he was a traditionalist and preferred the immaculate shiny black.

Grayson stared down as his order was placed in front of him, spreading across the table. It was the third day in a row that he had ordered a *full English* with extra toast, orange juice and a large filter coffee. A *Bakewell Tart* on the side for good measure. It wasn't that he was particularly hungry, he was simply setting out a large amount of food in front of him to justify sitting there for the better part of two-hours without raising suspicion. He wanted to gather as much information as he could. The first two days had resulted in little success. A casual passing comment here and there. He had no alternative, no other lead. He had been convinced that the conversation would be rife with opinion, theories and similar stories. Perhaps, if lucky, an insight into Mike Greenwood himself. Cabbies being known for their gossip and not holding back on their opinions.

Grayson was on the verge of giving up. Over an hour had passed and he was barely through a quarter of his breakfast, when Mike Greenwood walked into the cafe. There was a genuine rupture of surprise. A loud screech of wooden chairs on the tiled floor echoed around the room, as no less than nine assumed drivers stood to greet him. As he approached the group, the volume fell. There was an air of compassion in their welcoming, sympathetic shoulder pats and slow-firm hand-shakes followed sombre nods of acknowledgement. It was clear that this was the first time Greenwood had returned to the cafe since the incident.

When he was compiling a virtual file on Mike Greenwood, Grayson had often pictured confronting the man. The man that had killed Kamsi no less than a week earlier. He had assumed that he may need to visit him down the line, perhaps outside his house if needs must. In his mind he had built a picture of a stubborn, remorseless East Ender who might need a little persuasion to divulge his version of events. Perhaps with Joel at his side, for a little unspoken intimidation.

He watched him address his friends and colleagues. Clearly the incident had disturbed him. Compared to his *Facebook* photos, his skin looked gaunt with deep dark rings beneath his eyes.

Grayson took a slow sip of his now lukewarm coffee as he observed the group of men in front of him. After Greenwood had taken a seat, there was an awkward silence. By walking into the cafe, he would surely have expected to have to recall the events, but he seemed to struggle to find the opening words. A waiter placed a sandwich and mug in front of him, which broke the silence. Fried egg and sausage, Grayson assumed. With a milky tea and three sugars.

'If you or Kim need anything. Anything at all. You give me or my Kim a call. You hear?.' One man said to him. The man had a similar look to Greenwood, small in stature, thinning grey hair. He wore a neat green fleece and his accent indicated he was born within the sound of *Bow Bells*.

'Thanks John.'

The gesture seemed to place Mike at ease, or at least at ease enough to start his recollection of the event.

'She came out of nowhere.' Greenwood expressed as if starting a defence, but he had the empathy of his jury. He went on to calmly and methodically run through the events of the night.

'With Christmas around the corner and Kim and the girls out at the cinema, I thought I would work split hours. Three or four in the morning and seven or eight in the evening. Something like that. It was Friday see. As you fellas know, the nights can be eventful, but well, they're lucrative. Especially in December with all the office parties, people taking the cab all the way home rather than just to the station. Missed trains, longer fares'.

The group that surrounded him nodded in consensus, as he continued.

'I had gotten into the City at six o'clock. The early part of the evening had been mainly short runs. Waved down outside of bars and restaurants. The fares were mainly people rushing to mainline hubs, Kings Cross, Paddington, Victoria and the like. You know what its like, most rushing to get back to the families hours later than promised. Sitting on the edge of their seat, urging the taxi to defy traffic and get them to the stations early enough to avoid a drunken run or stumble to their train'.

The solemn concentration of his peers broke with a couple of wry smiles, but quickly re-engaged.

'It was just after ten, I picked up this couple from close to the *Shard*. They had been drinking at a pub in *Borough Market*. They wanted to go to Twickenham. A younger guy, perhaps early thirties. It was pretty clear he was going to be a guest at the older lady's house. She seemed to be in her fifties. His boss I reckon. Anyway, they begun the taxi journey cordially, but after ten minutes they were all over each other. Nothing you guys havn't seen a hundred, if not a thousand times before. I took them over London Bridge and along the Embankment, down the Mall, through Kensington, Hammersmith and across the river at Chiswick Bridge. Then through Kew and across Twickenham Bridge.'

'That's the route we all would have taken.' Reaffirmation coming from a thin Caribbean man sitting to Greenwood's side.

A lot of detail Grayson thought. Maybe force of habit when discussing driving routes. Maybe to garner credibility amongst his peers, both as a knowledgeable Cabbie and to illustrate a detailed recollection of the evening. Perhaps he was delaying having to recollect the moment the front left wing of his TX4 taxi struck and killed Kamsi.

'The streets down there were quiet, so I headed back into town. I decided to take Eastbound only, with half-a-mind to knock-it on-the-head completely.' He paused in thought. 'I wish I had.' Unfortunately, fate had different plans.

'As I reached Hyde Park Corner, at about midnight I guess, the heavens opened. So I thought I would dive into Covent Garden for one last fare.'

There was a general nod of understanding from the group. Rain would increase demand and make it easy to get a job, even one restricted solely to head East.

'It was torrential. Were you guys out in that?' One driver asked the group.

'I was. Absolutely pissing.' Another added as he nodded in agreement.

'On Shaftesbury Avenue, three girls got in. They were heading to that *Cargo* place, up in Hoxton. I dropped them on

Rivington Street and I called it a day. I switched off the light and was heading home, cutting up to Victoria Park by the Olympic Stadium.'

The group was now deeply engaged in the recollection. Grayson ensuring he took in every detail, using the techniques he had learnt as a kid, when he would remember the order of full packs of playing cards.

'I passed Cambridge Heath Station, onto Bishops Way. As I accelerated past the *Bestway* there, at the corner of what's it? Mowlem Street. That's it, Mowlem Street. She fell out into the road.' His voice inflected, palms upturned as he recalled his shock.

'Right in front of the taxi. I didn't have time to react.' Again he pleaded his case to the group, but from their reaction, it was clear they trusted his version of events.

'How did she manage to fall?' John asked.

'I'm not sure. She was a large lady. She fell pretty heavily. Maybe slipped on the wet pavement or twisted her ankle on the curb. She seemed to come out of nowhere.'

He paused as if trying to come up with answers to questions he had asked himself a hundred times or more.

'I don't know what more to say. The police agree it was an accident.'

'They accepted your word?' John asked, trying his hardest not to sound accusatory.

'I had my dash cam on. They took a copy of the video. It's a horrible sight, but it shows I was only doing 28 mph. And that she fell out of nowhere.'

Saying it out loud only exacerbated the look of distress on Mike Greenwood's face, as he once again had to face the fact that he had hit and killed a woman.

'Her name was Kamsiyonna. Kamsiyonna Olakunbi. A Nigerian lady. Apparently she worked at the *Cranbrook Community Centre*.'

With that he broke down. The Caribbean man providing a shoulder, before tears streamed from Mike Greenwoods eyes.

Grayson folded the newspaper in half, placed it on the table in front of him and maintained his focus on Mike Greenwood. He had a dash cam. He had seen them in plenty of *Uber* cars of late, but only a couple of times in Black Cabs. A video record of the whole incident. That must be the evidence the police officers on the case were referring to.

After about twenty minutes, the group had reduced to four. There was a genuine sense of camaraderie among the drivers, but bills still needed to be paid. Each departing driver gave Mike a word of support as they left. Other drivers had entered the cafe. They acknowledged Mike and the group, but didn't join. Grayson surmised that it was perhaps Greenwood's closest colleagues that had remained, willing to forgo an hour or two of fares to show their support. Although no less anxious in his demeanour, Greenwood seemed to hold confidence in the remaining men as he progressed the conversation.

'What about your Cab?' John asked. He had the more inquisitive look, but seemed to ask for the group.

'It's on my driveway. No damage. The police returned it yesterday after running a bunch of tests.'

Grayson listened in with mixed emotion. He had some sympathy for Mike, but was angry that they could wrap up an investigation up in under a week. A pure accident. Shut case.

'Truth is, I'm dreading it.' Mike said in soft admission. 'I'm not sure I will be able to get behind the wheel again, let alone drive. I can't sleep at night and keep seeing it over and over.' With a genuine look of exacerbation, he continued. 'But I don't know what to do. It's all I know. And we'll need the money. There's Abi's uni fees. Her accommodation and I'm still paying off the loan on the house extension.'

'It's a tough spot mate, but you'll get through it, you hear.'

'I know, I know. I'll have to.' Greenwood said. 'Well. I've taken up enough of your time. I'll let you get back to it.'

Mike Greenwood stood to leave. Grayson noticed that he had left half of his egg and bacon sandwich.

'I just thought I would come by. See some friendly faces. The missus, bless her, couldn't be more concerned, but I needed to get out of the house. You know?'

'If you are not in the cab I'll run you home.' One driver said.

'Thanks for the offer Terry, but I'd rather take the tube.'

'I understand mate. If you're sure. You take care, yeah. And we'll see you in here soon.'

Mike acknowledged the sentiment with a head nod and eye contact to each member of the group. He turned and ambled towards the door.

It took less than fifty yards for Grayson to catch up with Greenwood as he made his way from the cafe along Gresham Street, toward Bank Station and the Central line home.

He hadn't expected to encounter him in person. He trailed him, whilst he considered his opening approach. Polite and understanding? Firm and authoritative? Straight up threatening and aggressive?

As he passed the top of Wood Street, now out of sight of the *Piccolo Bar*, Greenwood's stature changed. No longer in a hunched slow dawdle, his pace had increased, taller, with a purpose. Convinced he hadn't been noticed Grayson scanned the busy street. Greenwood would have no reason to know who he was, even if he had recognised him from the cafe.

To his surprise, Greenwood made a sharp right on to Ironmonger Lane, a single lane that cut through to Cheapside. Although the direction was still towards Bank Station, the route he was now scurrying along was not the most direct. He then darted left into St. Olaves Court, a tiny passageway running due east.

Greenwood's sudden change of direction set Grayson back a few yards, compounded further by the increased pace. He tried to remain calm but panic began to set in as the passage took a tight turn and Greenwood slipped out of sight.

Grayson emerged from St. Olaves Court just in time to see a hurrying Greenwood descend into the Bank Station entrance.

He reached the Central Line Eastbound platform as the tube arrived. Mind on overdrive. Bank to Wanstead? About 25 minutes. Best carriage for the exit? Carriage five. Wait, why would Greenwood know that? He is a cabbie, not a commuter. Plus the fella seems to be on the run.

Squeezing between the bodies, he worked his way along scouring for Greenwood. Having covered only half of the platform when the high-frequency door-closing signal sounded, he jumped onto the tube. Confined to that carriage until the next stop.

As the tube pulled away towards Liverpool Street, Grayson took a moment to compose himself. There were three, maybe four carriages in front to check. He looked out through the dirt tinted window across to the Westbound platform, shocked to make out Mike Greenwood, cowering behind a pillared recess. He was staring intently back down the platform.

Grayson's Eastbound tube pulled away into the darkness of the tunnel.

19 HOUSE

A deafening screech, measured at over one-hundred decibels, gave passengers a harsh welcome to Bethnal Green. Train wheels scraping hard against the track as the carriages arced Eastwards. Faces grimaced at the high-pitch shrill. Lost in thought, it was barely audible to Grayson, who was trying to comprehend and deconstruct the morning's events. He had decided not to switch-back at Liverpool Street. If he did so, he would be too late to get back to Greenwood. In any case, he knew where he lived. He would stay on the Central Line through to Wanstead and wait, knowing that at some point he would have to return home.

As he exited the station, he cut across Christ Church Green to the corner of Chaucer Road and Addison Road. Although damp, grey and set against an overcast backdrop, the house was recognisable from Abigail Greenwood's sepia filtered *Instagram* posts. A 1960s, pebble-dashed semi-detached. Large bay window fronting a landscaped garden, a small rockery and well-kept lawn, bounded by tarred railway sleepers. The paved driveway was wide enough for two parked cars; however, only one occupied a space. It was the TX4, but unlike the photos from three years earlier, the 'Little Red Bus' no longer held a corporate sponsor, or so he thought on first glance. As Grayson looked closer he noted some white signage on the restored traditional black. A square logo depicting a building and arrows, with white text alongside that read, Point Developments: Reshaping the East End.

Within sight of the house Grayson held thirty yards back, standing against a wall in a position that only three houses overlooked, none of which shared a sight-line to Mike Greenwood's driveway. As he waited, he tried to account for everything said earlier at *Piccolos Cafe*. He considered the timings set-out by Mike Greenwood and every statement he had made. And as if sat at the poker table, he reviewed every action and reaction, from every member of the group. He was looking for any hidden truth subconsciously conveyed.

Everything told him that Mike Greenwood would not be a strong card player. There was no bluffing. His recollection of events was truthful and his remorse genuine. Grayson had no doubt about this, but standing there outside the man's house, he had to consider why he shot off into Bank station and did not head home. He interrogated his review of Greenwood. From the moment he had walked into the cafe, Grayson had viewed him through the lens of a broken, innocent man, with no reason not to tell a true tale of events. Perhaps, he considered, something was missing, a part of the story withheld?

There was a nagging annoyance. At first, he couldn't identify the source, but as he reviewed the events of the morning, he reached the origin of his frustration in the form of a simple question. Why had Mike Greenwood visited the cafe? He had heard Greenwood's version, 'to get away from the missus'. Maybe it was a valid reason, maybe he needed a break from daytime TV and couldn't stand to look at the vehicle in the driveway. Maybe he wanted to express his innocence to his peers and maybe he wanted to see his friends, but something didn't sit right.

Maybe, just maybe he wanted to show someone he was acting normally.

Grayson stood motionless, leaning against a wall as he ran through every question he could construct. What was he not disclosing? What was he trying to prove?

Over an hour past. There had been no sign of Greenwood's return and no movement in the house. Grayson's robust patience was wearing thin. His thoughts had led him away from Greenwood, to the taxi cab that sat on the driveway.

He wanted to take a closer look. Although confident it was, he rang the doorbell to ensure the house was empty and was relieved that no-one answered. He had every intention of looking over the entire vehicle, but as he approached, only one thing drew his attention. The dash-cam sitting in the window.

The rush of adrenaline upon seeing the dash-cam spurred him into action. He took a cursory look around to ensure there were no curtain twitchers prying on him, nor any home security cameras pointing in his direction. Picking up a fist-sized stone from the rockery, he took a crouched position between the taxi and the house. Reaching up, with one swift strike, he smashed the driver's side window. To his surprise, the smash was not met with the sound of an alarm. With his hand in his sleeve, he unlocked and opened the door and reached for the dash-cam, disconnecting it from its mount and power wire. He placed it in his pocket, closed the door and exited the driveway, turning the corner, to the visual cover of the wall running along the side of the property.

Heading back to the tube station across Christ Church Green, he paused and took cover behind a tree. He pulled the dash-cam from his pocket and studied the device. It was like the mini cameras he associated with action sports.

A look round to ensure he was alone and out of sight, he turned the device on. The screen showed a live stream of the tree roots at his feet. He pressed the top button bringing up a menu and selected the second listed option, 'play'. The screen was black, with a small white time stamp in the corner. The date read 9/12/2017 and time 17:32.07. He again pressed the top button to start the video. The time ticked, second-by-second, 17:32.08, 17:32:09, 17:32.10. At first, he thought the footage was blank, but from the small speaker he heard a cough and then the screen lit up as the headlights of the taxi illuminated the Greenwood's driveway and the house opposite.

20 HIT

18 DECEMBER 2017

In the small kitchen space, Grayson stood over a table that pinned two chairs against the wall. On the table sat a *MacBook*, a large road map of London and an open pack of coloured marker pens.

He had plugged the dash-cam into the *MacBook* over thirty minutes earlier. That was the easy bit. And whilst the over preparation of materials had momentarily calmed him, his nerves were now back to heightened levels. He paced the room and took deep breaths as he willed himself to do what was right. To be strong and press on with his investigation.

He pictured his life with Kamsi. That first smile she gave him as he walked arm-in-arm with Ama into the Community Centre. Her open embrace as he ran to her in the new home on the Estate. Her laughter whilst the four of them sat at the dining table at their flat. When he and Joel had got into trouble, she had always been the good cop, the consoling, understanding, encouraging and doting auntie. Memories of Kamsi scrolled in his thoughts like a highlight real. Each moment more vivid than the last, coming to rest at the sight of her standing on the stage two weeks earlier, concern and love for her residents. She beamed with pride as she concluded her presentation.

He continued to pace back and forth, trying to build the courage to press play, knowing what he would see would be horrid, and once seen, it could not be unseen.

He had gone through the timeline of his movements that evening over and over. Interrogated his memory to the greatest extent, noting every detail he could remember from the moment he left his apartment towards the *Acorn* pub. He had spent the afternoon making detailed notes of every piece of evidence he could. The text message to Piers to swap the holdalls, sent at 10:12. An initial receipt at 10:58 for drinks at NT's and a later one at 23:45. There was a *WhatsApp* message to Sofia sent at 00:14 as they exchanged phone numbers. Although irrelevant he had noted the time of Piers' *WhatsApp* messages, after he and Tessa had parted company with Grayson and Sofia. They were either messages expressing gratitude for the night, or messages that graphically detailed what he planned to get up to with Tessa.

After he had set out his own actions that evening, he started on a list of questions regarding Kamsi's movements, but seven, or eight questions in and he realised that only the first one mattered.

What was she doing out at that time of the morning?

He had concluded he had seen her at 00:45 as his taxi made a right turn onto Mare Street. That was the time at which the bus passed. The number D6, pulling away from the stop, perhaps a minute or two earlier than the scheduled

00:46 time according to the TFL website.

Detective Cullen had, reluctantly, provided some outline information upon closing the police investigation. Greenwood had made the call to the emergency services at 00:56, requesting an ambulance. Based on the information received the operator ensured the dispatch of both ambulance and the police. They had arrived in unison six minutes after they received the call.

Grayson used the marker pens to plot all the timelines on the map and stuck a series of *post-it notes* in different locations, with differing comments, times or questions. He had printed photos of Greenwood and his taxi, sourced from *Facebook* and *Instagram*. He had listed the clothing that Kamsi had been wearing that night.

Having exhausted every line of information he could, he knew he had to watch the dash-cam footage. He couldn't put it off any longer. He had no desire to watch it, but he needed to know more. He could not accept that this was an accident. There was too much strangeness to the scenario of Kamsi being there, the tragic coincidence that he had seen her that night and Squelch's phone call. Equally as troubling was the question why Greenwood hadn't returned home in the hour or so he had waited.

There must be more to it. The police may have closed their investigation, but Grayson's was barely underway.

He couldn't press play. He reached for a whisky bottle and thick-bottomed glass that sat on the kitchen counter. As his pour reached a single measure, he up-ended the bottle, filling over half the glass, before returning the bottle to the counter.

In the first drink, he emptied most of the contents. In an immediate second go, he finished the glass, refilling it before placing it on the table in front of him. He drank directly from the bottle, two or three large swigs.

From the counter he retrieved a pen and paper to make a timeline of the six hour, forty minute video. He would make note of every detail, pick-up and drop-off times, routes between locations, the traffic, client-driver conversations, the music on the radio, Greenwood's phone calls and the weather conditions. He took another hit of whisky as he mustered the courage to open the file. Through gritted teeth, he pressed play.

The glass smashed against the wall.

'Fuuuuck!' He yelled from the pit of his stomach.

He couldn't watch anymore.

Grimacing, he stumbled backwards, the wall bracing him as his legs lost strength. He slid down, body tucking behind buckled knees, empty bottle in hand. He could no longer hold back the tears, smuttering as his resistance failed.

Initially, the camera gave a wide perspective and high level of detail, but from about midnight, specifically 00:06.22 on the clock onwards, the heavy rain and peripheral misting of the windows narrowed the view considerably. Further restricted by the fast-moving wipers and heavy rain that beat against the windscreen. By the time of the collision, the dash-cam's field of vision was only two metres from the front of the taxi and barely covered the width of the headlights.

Following the collision, Kamsi's body lay in the road, below the view of the dash-cam. Greenwood was in centre view, crouched by her side. He made an attempt to talk to her before he reached for his mobile and called an ambulance. The dash-cam only recorded audio of the heavy rain that struck the windscreen. His face in panic, he continuously scoped his location and appeared to be answering the operator's questions. His head paused as he focused off to his right, as if reading the street sign and relaying the information to the operator.

The ambulance arrived after six minutes. It was clear by the Paramedic's reaction that Kamsi was already lost.

Trying to find any detail that may help explain the incident, Grayson had watched the lead-up over twenty times. The impact itself probably fifty. At full speed, the high-pitched screeching of wet breaks was met with the dreadful sound of the front left wing of the cab making the impact. At half-speed, he noticed the trajectory of Kamsi's fall into the road, horizontal as she entered the view. And frame-by-frame, Kamsi's eyes stared horrified at the taxi moments before it hit her. The image would forever haunt him. Her eyes were also his last thought before he slumped to the ground and passed out.

The dulling pain in his shoulder brought him to consciousness. The second eye-opening in delay to the first. Pushing himself upright from the floor he began to draw focus. The laptop screen in front of him was bright. Frozen on a frame of the video.

Squinting at the screen, he attempted to shut the laptop, missing on his first swipe. As he reached out for a second time, he paused. The angle of the shot was the same as he had reviewed, but something had caught his eye. Or someone.

He took a moment to compose himself, open his eyes fully and ensure the function of his senses. The subconscious indicators materialised into conscious view. A shot of vivid red hair. There, in the centre-right of the screen, at the back of a small gathered group. It was Lloyd Blake.

21 ACTION

He thought he would go to Joel straight away. He pictured the moment when he would sit him down and tell him that Lloyd Blake had been at the site minutes after Kamsi had been killed. This would certainly add to his grief, but he knew his friend too well. Of greater concern was that he would have no way to control Joel's anger. Grayson decided he would first have to understand his own reaction. He too was still in pain, guilt and a deep state of shock that Kamsi had been taken. He pushed through clouded thoughts and tried not to jump immediately to conclusions, but it didn't sit right. It was too much of a coincidence. On the same night that Blake had been an accomplice in stealing, or at least trying to steal one-hundred and fifty thousand pounds from him, he ends up at the site of Kamsi's death. Then there was

Squelch's phone call.

Yes, he had a long and turbulent history with Lloyd Blake, not only at school but also on the estate. Kamsi too had her run-ins with Blake over the years, most notably when she caught him red-handed graffitiing the side of the Community Centre. Grayson had suggested that he and Joel teach Blake a lesson, but Kamsi had pleaded for him not to after the trouble that had occurred at school. Blake knew that Kamsi was close with Grayson, practically family, but to consider his involvement in her death, that was surely too much of a stretch. And from everything he had unfortunately seen on the dash-cam footage, Kamsi had fallen into the street and was struck by Greenwood's taxi. Yet he was there.

He couldn't go to the Police. They would only question how Grayson obtained the video in the first place. By now Greenwood surely would have reported the broken window and stolen dash-cam. The bottom line, Grayson determined, was that getting Joel involved would create too much risk and too many ancillary problems, but he had questions. He needed to get the full picture. He would have to go and pay a visit to Blake alone and get some answers.

Residents of Offenbach am Main, to the east of Frankfurt, may be embarrassed to know Bethnal Green is twinned with their district. They would certainly be dismayed if they saw *Offenbach House*, at the centre of the *Cranbrook Estate*, carrying their namesake to celebrate the union. The brutalist style tower, completed in the early 1960's to much celebration, had seen little upgrade since.

Grayson had watched Lloyd Blake and Ryan Walsh enter the building two hours earlier. Flat 46, on the twelfth floor was home to Blake and his mother. They had moved in shortly after his birth, with no father figure to speak of. Over the years several men had kept the company of Linda Blake, never lasting more than a few months at a time. Her hostile temper, often fuelled by gin and vodka, combined with the troublesome ginger bastard she came with, were all too often convenient excuses for the men to leave.

Outside of the flat, Grayson waited in the stairwell's darkness. The post-war modernist design and wrought iron balustrades gave him a view to the doors of all four flats on the floor. Moments after midnight, Walsh emerged from the flat and made his way across to the elevator. Grayson sat in silence and waited for him to descend and exit through the main door. The noise of the closing latch echoed up the stairwell. He made his way to the flat and double tapped the door, in a manner that might suggest it was Walsh returning.

As the door opened, Grayson burst through, grabbed Blake by the scruff-of-the-neck with his left hand and struck him in the face three times in quick succession with his right. He dragged him from the flat and tipped him up over the balustrade, holding him over the twelve-story drop.

'Give me a reason that I don't end you right here and now, you little prick!'

Blake, helpless to fight back, was in panic and could not put together a coherent answer.

Grayson pushed him further over the balustrade, now beyond the horizontal.

'Just... just...put me up.' Blake stuttered.

Grayson shook him. Arms burning under the weight, but for now, adrenaline gave him the strength to hold him in place.

Blake's breathing was panicked, blood streamed from his nose.

'Er... er...er.'

'Don't fucking 'er' me. What the fuck were you doing there?' Grayson snarled through gritted teeth.

Blake, stretched out in fear, he failed to gather any

purchase, resigned himself to his helpless position and managed just, to string a sentence together.

'Er… It was Squelch. His idea. Him and James Johnson.'

'I asked what you were doing there?!'

'Er…stop… Fuck!… Just… er…look… He only brought me in to the game to wind you up. Fuck with you. You know, distract you. I didn't know any more than that… I swear.' His voice strained under stress.

'I mean, I knew he wanted to do you over… But didn't know how.' Blake still inverted, still terrified, somehow managed to show some fight. Or stupidity.

'You know he'll get to you and fuck you up.'

Grayson ignored the comment. Growing with intensity, he leaned forward and pulled Blake's face up close to his.

'I am going to ask you this once, and once only. If you give me some bullshit answer, it's night-night-no-biscuit for you.' He pushed Blake back below the horizontal. 'Now tell me you understand!'

'Yeah, I understand. Fuck!' Blake yelled.

In a slow, clear voice, Grayson asked.

'What were you doing on Bishops Way on Friday night?

The question stunned Blake. His face was red as blood rushed downwards to his head, sweat beads forming across his brow. A vein bulging from his forehead.

'Kamsi! What did you do to Kamsi?' Grayson yelled.

Blake's realisation set in.

His face now lined with concern. Concern that Grayson believed he had something to do with Kamsi's death.

'Mate, it wasn't us!'

Grayson could detect the smallest trace of empathy in his reaction.

'What wasn't you? Why were you there?'

'Look… look, just… just put me down, put me down and I'll tell you.' Blake begged.

More in conceit to his burning arms than Blake's plea, Grayson pulled him back upright, until his feet found ground. He did not release his two-handed grip to Blake's collar, keeping his back pressed up against the balustrade.

'Talk,' he demanded.

'Look. Squelch sent us out to find you. You are fucking dead by the way.'

'You worry about yourself.'

'Squelch sent us out to find you.'

'Who's us?' Grayson knew full well he was referring to Walsh, but laid the test anyway.

'Me and Walsh.' Blake answered. First test passed.

'We had been back to the *Acorn*, and found the backdoor to your safe. Prick.' He couldn't help himself. 'We saw Kamsi out on the High Street. We thought.'

'You *think* now do you?'

'Fucking odd seeing her out at that time of night. And she was carrying these bags. We thought it was the cash from the safe and she was bringing it to you. So we followed her.'

Grayson's stare did not falter. Breathing through gritted teeth. Blake continued.

'We followed for 10 minutes, probably less. As she walked past *Bestway*, it looked like she turned on to... what's it?'

'Mowlem Street.' Grayson impatiently answered.

'Yeah, that's it. We were well behind her, but as we come up to the corner, she fell out into the road, right in front of a taxi'

'What do you mean she just fell out?'

'It was dark, pissing with rain. We couldn't see clearly but she just stumbled and fell out into the road, right as the taxi went by. We stopped where we were. The taxi driver jumped straight out and was looking at her. He got on his mobile and a few minutes later the ambulance and police arrived.'

The fear had got to Blake, his face paler than ever, border

line translucent. There was no way he was making this up Grayson determined.

'We got closer. The Ambulance people were trying to help, but she was dead. You could see it.'

Grayson didn't want to believe him. He wanted to throw him over the balustrade there and then. Be done with this irritant for good, but he could tell Blake was far too scared to be lying.

He released the grip on his collar and shoved him backwards, snarling in frustration. He was considering the next steps, when Blake broke the silence.

'The weirdest thing though... the bags she had. They were gone.'

22 CARD

His growing frustration made the slow descent of the elevator even more painful. The adrenaline had subsided, but nervous tension maintained his high heart rate as he contemplated the fact that his intuition had been right. There was something more to Kamsi's death than just an accident, but he didn't know what.

There was no doubt in his mind that Blake had, albeit under duress, given him a truthful version of what he had seen that evening. The main question of why Kamsi was out that late was now compounded by additional questions. Why did she have those bags? What was in them? And where had they gone?

He half expected to see Squelch on the ground floor as the elevator doors opened. He had taken Blake's mobile phone.

And for good measure permanently disconnected the internet in the flat when he smashed the modem. He knew just as soon as he could, Blake would contact Squelch and inform him of the visit. He would have to deal with that another time. For now, his priority was to find out what Kamsi was doing that night.

As he walked along the concrete pathway, away from *Offenbach House* towards the Bethnal Green gate, he looked across the estate to Ama's block. A soft glow from the fifth-floor window of the flat informed him that the reading light in the lounge was on, which meant she was awake. She now suffered only a couple of hours sleep a night.

Contrite and feeling drained from the events of the day, his thoughts went to Ama and the torture she was putting herself through, as she grieved the death of her sister. He knew he should comfort her and turned back to her building.

He sent a text as he approached, letting Ama know he was on his way up. With no immediate response, rather than let himself in, he knocked gently so as not to startle her. To his surprise, having read the text, she met him at the door on the first knock. He had expected to see her how she had been in the days prior, tired, fearful and upset. Whilst she did look exhausted, Grayson detected a subtle change in her manner, a determined glint in her eyes. As he took off his jacket and hung it on the hook behind the door he looked across to the dining table. On it, sat high piles of the cards and tributes that had adorned the Community Centre fence.

'I didn't want the weather to ruin them,' she said picking a card from the top of a pile and moving to the sofa and the reading light to review the words written within.

'People are kind,' she continued.

A simple statement, but given what Ama was going through, the words said as much about the reader as those who laid the tribute. She had latched on to a small grain of solace and positivity. Grayson could only admire her strength.

'There is so much pain in the world Grayson.' Her eyes sought for understanding in his.

Sometimes Ama's conviction in her faith made Grayson reconsider his indifference to religion.

'Kamsi is with the Lord now. She need not suffer this world any longer.' She said, passing him a newspaper from the side-table.

Grayson tried to comprehend the resignation and sadness that had crossed Ama's face. Perhaps it was a further stage of grief, but could not determine if she had made a positive step.

He perched on the sofa next to Ama and looked at the paper, which was folded open to page four. It was a copy of *The Nation*, a Nigerian newspaper that made it to London, a week or so after going to print. He remembered, when he was younger, Kamsi would read the paper in detail once a week. Sometimes she made a specific trip to a shop in Peckham in a rush to pick up a copy before the news got any older. She would always return with a bag full of yams and spices and set to work in the kitchen. As she read page-by-page she would fill the flat with an incredible aroma. Kamsi always longed for Nigeria, her hometown and people. Ama had often said it was because she had been too young to truly remember the devastation they had witnessed before they fled.

To momentarily distract Ama from her grief, Talisa, a church friend, had brought by the paper. Unfortunately, Talisa had not read the contents before passing it to her. Across pages 4 and 5 was a detailed report of extensive Christian bloodshed in Northern Nigeria. Modern-day terrorism, carried out in the name of Islam, by Boko Haram and Fulani tribesmen, with the death count now in the thousands. For Ama it was a horrific reminder of the events that had led them to flee to London in the early '90s, leaving behind everything they had ever known. In that moment, it became clear to Grayson that she truly felt Kamsi was now in a better place, where no further pain or suffering could reach her.

'I understand,' he said. A small moment of closure, but grief isn't so easily navigated. As Ama's tiredness began to win over, a resistance emerged.

'I don't know what she was doing out so late?' She exclaimed. 'She never would be out that late. And even if she was, it would only be down at the Community Centre.'

Grayson hadn't intended to bring Ama into his investigation, but he had no answers for her and had nowhere else to turn.

'Ama.' Grayson said, as softly as possible. 'I don't want to upset you further, but I have to ask you something.'

Ama said nothing but gave Grayson a look as if to suggest that nothing he could say could upset her any further.

'I have some information that wasn't in the police report.' Noting her comprehension he continued.

'On that night, Kamsi had some bags with her. Some large plastic woven travel bags.'

Ama understood his reference. She stood and walked to a small built-in cupboard next to the kitchen door. She unlatched and opened the door before searching through the bottom shelf, rifling through the contents.

'They're gone!' She said, seeming surprised, 'we had three, maybe four bags here, but they're gone.'

'Ok, ok,' Grayson said, not knowing where his line of inquiry was going. 'What was in the bags?'
The question perplexed Ama.

'In them? Nothing was in them, they were empty. We used them for shopping and things like that. Why did she have those bags with her?'

'I'm not sure,' Grayson said, 'but after the accident, the bags were gone. Someone must have taken them. Someone must have been there.'

Ama's mind raced to keep up with what Grayson was suggesting.

'Ama. I'm not sure she fell.'

Taken aback, Ama took time to process. She wouldn't doubt him, but grappled to comprehend the consequences of the statement.

'Everybody loved her. Why would anybody want to hurt her?' She tailed off the question with a shudder. A look of realisation. Then panic.

'No!' She began shaking her head. 'No, no, no!'

She broke down, her head buried, wailing into Grayson's shoulder.

After, what seemed like an eternity she calmed a little. Her heart and head still racing she began to pull together a coherent sentence.

'The Community Centre.'

Grayson looked at her, confused.

'The argument.'

'What argument?' Grayson asked with concerned urgency.

'The man at the Community Centre.'

Grayson urged her to continue.

'He was shouting at us. He shouted at Kamsi. He said that she was lying. That we wouldn't stand in their way.'

'What do you mean Ama? What man? When?'

'At the meeting. At the end. Three men at the back stood up and one started shouting,' she continued, 'they were not from the Estate, they were dressed differently. Smartly dressed.'

Ama began to take deep breaths, she focused and tried not to hyperventilate.

'He was angry, not aggressive, but threatening, like in a superior way. He argued against Kamsi's presentation. He said she was wrong and it was good for the Estate to be sold. That it would improve the area for the residents.'

'Kamsi argued back. Some of the residents came to her defence. It went on for a few minutes, until Pastor Okereke told the man to return to his seat. Then he thanked everyone for coming.'

Ama reached for a glass of water. She took a sip to calm herself before she continued.

'Afterwards. Once most people had left, they came up to us. Well two of them did, the younger ones and,' she paused, to gather her thoughts, 'I mean, they were polite, but.'

'What Ama?'

'They. Well, they were, what's the word? Patronising. Patronising, that's it.'

She studied Grayson for his comprehension.

'Surely they wouldn't have done anything to Kamsi.'

'Where were they from?' Grayson said.

'I don't know,' she said, now visually anxious, 'English, I think.'

'Sorry, Ama. I mean did they say if they worked for anyone?'

Ama reached for her handbag.

'Here.' She said as she retrieved an item from the bag and handed it to Grayson.

'They gave me a business card.'

23 TURN

He urged himself through the darkness along the path out of the estate. Lifeless light fell to the empty road. Well past midnight, no late-night runners, no passing cars or buses. Buildings stood dark. The streets exhausted, sapped of all energy. Every step he took was heavy.

A westbound train clattered away as he approached Bethnal Green station. The information board showed 14 mins until the next and final train. His mind was too active, he had to keep moving.

Streetscapes of shadows, noises were distant.

On Roman Road, he passed the large red doors of the old fire station. He ran his hand along the damp brickwork. His head fell, vision tunnelled to the glistening pavement no more than five yards ahead. Memories flashed.

As a six-year-old he imagined those doors bursting open, a shiny red engine flying out. A hand on his shoulder, his dad's. He smiled down at him and ruffled his hair as he explained that the firemen were no longer there. Now in their new station on the other side of the road.

His legs continued to pace, fuelled on fumes of adrenaline. Coherent thoughts were hard to compile. He could not comprehend how someone could wish harm to Kamsi.

The first drops of rain fell as he paced down Whitechapel Road. His mind spun. His dad's voice was still present. He encouraged him to keep up, not to get distracted by the bustle outside the *East London Mosque*, or the trader-calls coming from the street market opposite. His waist-high vision awash with colours, movement, flashes of steam and smoke.

Those streets now empty, skeletons of dismantled stall frames and shuttered shopfronts. Bin men and street cleaners the guardians of the night. He struggled to keep pace and stumbled on a cracked paving slab. He reached for his dad, but he was not there.

At Aldgate, he cut into the back alleys. He had to keep moving. Why had he not gone back for Kamsi? The static noise of rainwater pounded the pavement, blocked drains and low filling curbs. A lone night-walker passed under the streetlight, head dipped under the hood of his raincoat.

He weaved through the dark narrow lanes. A distrusting iron gate guarded the blackness beyond. Distant sirens echoed and reverberated under the platforms at Fenchurch Street. He emerged at All Hallows Church where cars rushed past, pooled rainwater ejected in all directions.

As he stepped on to the bridge, his vision was back with his dad. The burst of excitement as he released his hand. He was free to run. He dodged in and out of passers-by. His cheeks ached, giddy with excitement. Short of breath he arrived at the mid-point of the bridge. He reached up to the rail with both hands and aligned his head to the gap in the granite wall. The best view.

A bus slowed. Low lights illuminated the desolate souls, faces pressed to the window staring to the sodden street below.

The rail is much lower now. It chilled to touch as rainwater soaked into his sleeve. His heart pounds as he realises the visions were of *that* day. The last time they set out on the daily three mile adventure. He panned across the bridge to the looming tower of Guy's Hospital and the low light of the oncology ward on the fourteenth floor. It took him back to that mid-summer morning.

He knew the way. Second corridor on the right, fourth room on the left. He retrieved his drawing from his rucksack as he scuttled off. He had worked on it until bedtime, then spent extra time that morning to get the details just right. He could not wait to give the drawing to his mum. It was their house on Old Ford Road, with a large tree in the garden and the fire station next door. Of course, there were firemen inside, by their shiny red truck. Next to the house was Ama, and Grayson, mum and dad smiling as they held hands. Like they used to do, like they would soon do again. For the first time she was not sat up in her bed when he arrived. He paused, unsure if he should go in. His dad caught up, and they entered. He climbed up onto the chair next to the bed and began to show mum his picture.

His lungs stung, his chest coursed. He grasped to the rail, his legs took support from the frozen granite. He focused on the black water below and tried to control his breaths. A dagger of guilt, as he recalled those last moments with his mum, frustrated that she didn't look at his drawing. She wouldn't talk to him, she just laid there. And she had missed his birthday. He was too young to know. Too young to understand that her cancer had spread rapidly and had been detected too late. He had not understood why his dad smiled as he clasped her hand. Too young to differentiate between a genuine look of happiness and one compelled by his wish to make the last moments with his wife less harrowing.

As his mum's gaze moved to his dad, he saw his smile evaporate, in its place, panic. Suddenly an arm swept him from the chair up on to the bed, his chest and face pulled firmly against his mum. His dad squeezed them tighter, the grip and pressure overwhelmed him.

The shock stunned him, he could not react. After what seemed like an eternity, the grip subsided. He slid from the side of the bed and found weak footing as his knees buckled. His wish to cry was halted by the wail his dad let out. Nurse Ama moved quickly into the room and as urgently as his dad had swept him from the chair, she picked Grayson up and pulled him tight to her chest. She wept as she held him. His mum had held on for one last moment to see her boys, but now was gone.

Teeth clenched and lips fused, his nostrils pulsed cold jets of breath. His back shuddered. The tears stung as they froze to his cheek. He could no longer stand. The metal railing slid from his elbows to wrists, as his knees dropped to the concrete and forehead came to rest on the granite wall. Moments later he collapsed to the ground.

The bone-deep cold brought him round. Not sure how long he was out. Comprehension was slow, as he failed to grasp the wall before reaching to the railing above. He shivered as he painfully pulled himself upright and gained an unnerving footing. The blurred glow of an orange taxi light drew his attention as it turned onto the bridge and came towards him. With a final surge of energy he threw an arm up to hail the cab and let out an incomprehensible gasped yelp. The driver swerved into the inside lane and accelerated past him. Grayson collapsed back to the ground. His arm gave way. He toppled, striking his left shoulder. He thought of his mum. Then his last conscious thought was of Kamsi, as his cheek lay on the frozen concrete.

24 RAGGED

He woke to a low tone hum coming from a machine next to the bed. A vignette of fluorescent white light spun as he opened his eyes. A nurse spoke to him. Her tone was soft and warm, but her words were distant, they did not register. As she concluded and left, he scanned the stark pale room. He always associated hospitals with emptiness and loss.

He laid still and tried to rationalise the loss of Kamsi, weighing up his pain against the guilt of leaving her in the cold. He wasn't to know what would happen, but that didn't make it any easier to bear. For a moment he began to comprehend what his father must have felt the day his mother died. The grief of losing someone so close, the guilt that they pass, but you live on. Until that day, his father had been his hero, his protector. With a blink of an eye, it was over. Love and protection replaced with dissolution and despair.

He wanted to believe he was different. Stronger. He wouldn't let grief drive him to abandon those he loved. He gathered his focus and strength to sit up and removed the drip from his arm. It took him a moment to find his feet as he stood and recovered his clothes. He was quick to dress and slip out of the room.

As he paced past the nurses station, they called for him to wait, to see the doctor. Undeterred he shot through the exit door in to the stairwell, down three flights and out on to the street. In his rush he hadn't stopped to consider in which hospital he had woken.

Disoriented, he scanned the street. Evening drizzle turning heavy. Cars and taxis flew bye. A red bus lurched towards him, before coming to rest at a bus stop a yard or so in front. Passengers pushed passed him to board. As he turned to locate the hospital signage, the sight of the scaffold clad Big Ben across the river caught his eye. The landmark told him he was at St Thomas's. So to get where he was going, he headed towards Waterloo underground station.

♠

He hesitated before he eventually rang the bell. Beyond the glass, bright colours moved towards the door. He recognised the burgundy. As soon as the winter rolled in Estella would recover his old sweater from the back of the wardrobe, to throw on with a pair of baggy ripped jeans and thick socks.

As she swung open the door, she tailed off a call.

'It's Grayson, I've gotta go. Say hi to dad for me. Love ya.'

'Hey,' she said, her expression was soft.

In that instant he didn't wish to be there, he wanted to

back away, turn and run. Leave her the way she was, perfect. Sensing his unease, she reached out and pulled him close. Her arms wrapped high, as his head fell to her shoulder.

'I'm so sorry,' she said as she pulled him tighter. With every passing second her embrace quashed his anxiety, before she finally released and looked at him, her eyes welling.

'She was an amazing woman. I couldn't believe it when I heard. I still don't. How did she? Sorry,' she stepped aside, 'Come in.'

He tentatively accepted the invitation and stepped into the hallway.

'Come and sit down.' Estella said, leading him into the lounge where soft furnishings lined the sofa, lit candles and a thick novel lay half open on the coffee table, next to a large glass of red wine.

He hung in the doorway.

'No, thanks, it's ok, I shouldn't have come.'

'But you did and I'm glad you did. How are you? How's Ama?'

'She's strong, coping you know, but this, this is different.'

'I can't imagine. They were so close. It must be horrific.'

'I'm hoping the funeral will help. It's the day after tomorrow. You should come.'

Her hand reached out to his.

'Look. You know I cared for Kamsi, but I don't think its right that I come. Ama needs you and given everything between us right now, I don't want to be a distraction.'

He gave her an understanding nod.

'I meant what I said. With all that's going on, with Kamsi and everything, I'm here for you, but when it comes to us, I need time. You understand?'

'Yeah,' he said with resignation 'I understand.'

'Look, I shouldn't have come. I just…'

He looked around the room. Tranquil and calm.

'I'm going to go, yeah. I'll see you soon.'

'You don't have to leave. Stay a while.'

He wanted to. He wanted to tell her everything. That Kamsi's death hadn't been an accident, that he was going to do everything he could to find out who killed her, but seeing her unburdened by him and his issues, he couldn't. In that moment it become clear.

'I've got to go.' He said, with urgency.

'There's some things I've got to do.'

She stood to stop him, but he had made his move to the door.

'Sorry.' He said, as he rushed out.

As he paced along the street a shot of adrenaline surged through his body, fuelling a resolve. He couldn't turn to Joel. He had no way of controlling his reaction to the fact that days after being confronted at the Community Centre Kamsi had been killed, that Squelch had laid down a threat towards Ama, that Lloyd Blake had been at the scene of Kamsi's death, or that he was now sure that there had been someone there that night, at the moment that she went into the road and was struck by Greenwood's taxi.

It was too much for Joel to be burdened with. It was too much for himself to comprehend. He also knew he had no answers to give Joel as to why Squelch would threaten Ama. He couldn't stomach the thought of amplifying the lie, nor trying to explain why moments before her death, he had left Kamsi out there in the rain. Joel was, and had always been his conscience, and at that moment, he daren't face him.

He thought of going to the police, but what would he say? That based on some missing bags he was sure that someone was there when Kamsi fell into the road. That probably she didn't fall, but was pushed in front of that taxi, but nobody saw the push, nor who had pushed her. Or that he had a theory of motive, based on a business card and voiced opposition in a public meeting. The police officer would laugh him out of the station.

At the very least the police would want to know how he came across such information. Sure, he could point them to his source, but what good would that do? No way would they open up a murder inquiry on the word of an estate urchin-like Lloyd Blake. And even if they believed him, he was sceptical to think they would stretch their scarce resources to reopen an already closed case, especially one involving the death of a black asylum recipient in the East End.

He also had to consider that he wouldn't want the Police investigating how he learnt that Lloyd Blake was at the scene. Breaking into Greenwood's taxi to steal his dash-cam. Nor having to edge around the fact that he had seen Kamsi minutes before she was killed, but didn't seem to care enough to help her and pick her up. No, Grayson concluded, if he wanted to find the truth, to investigate this firm and these individuals, he would have to do it himself.

25 BUY

He addressed the third and final invitation to Henry Sloane, Vice President of Acquisitions. The very same Henry Sloane who was acquainted with Piers Fitzgerald-Smithe and had been loose-lipped enough to tell Piers of their plans for the estate. Grayson studied the business card. Thick weight, off-white, high-quality silver etched with an embossed font. The logo, a simple, but assertive arrow-head, mono-tone black with the company name in a formal serif font, which read, Black Spear Group Inc.

As he spun the card between thumb and forefinger, he considered the question that had been playing on his mind since he lay in the hospital bed the day before. Could such a firm be capable of murder? To kill someone who posed only a minor bump-in-the-road to the fulfilment of their plan. Given the multi-million-pound stakes of the deal and the impact disgruntled tenants could have, he did not like the conclusion he reached.

Ama had identified Sloane's two colleagues when Grayson showed her a series of head-shots printed from the corporate website. They too would receive one of the invitations he had now placed on the table. He would hand-deliver the invitations to the Black Spear office reception to ensure they reached the recipients before they fled for the festive holidays. Professionally printed, envelopes handwritten for a personal touch. The words 'exclusive invitation' on the corner so they wouldn't be discarded with the hundreds of Christmas cards circulating the office.

He knew the plan was crude at best, but given the little time he had, it would have to do. The invitations were addressed from Piers Fitzgerald-Smithe of Howell Spencer Stokes LLP. Piers often told Grayson that these types of guys get-off on debaucherous behaviour and in his words, 'would turn up to the opening of an envelope, if it involved champagne and coke.' From his brief research into the three individuals, Grayson thought Piers' assessment to be correct.

He took a step back from the table to widen his perspective and piece-by-piece interrogate his research so far. As a child he had spent years isolated in his room running through number patterns and playing cards. Visualisation, that was how he best processed information, so that is what he turned to. He had made a display of notes, maps and photographs set out across the wall. Times and places drawn with marker pen or linked with string. The display helped him visualise the night of December 9th, to get into the head of others, Greenwood, Blake and Kamsi to better understand their movements and motives.

Picking up the three photos, he stuck them to a clear space on the wall. Beneath each individual, he placed bulleted information about the three men who had been at the *Cranbrook Community Centre* meeting. Their job titles, roles, backgrounds. He reviewed publications, corporate and social media. Where possible he mapped out their family ties and relationships. All in an attempt to gain insight before he confronted them.

As it stood, that was Grayson's plan. To engineer a meeting where he could get a read on these men. Find out if to close a deal they were capable of premeditated murder. He wanted to get them in a social context, disarm them with alcohol and give the entertainment some locational relevance. For that reason, the invitations set out an itinerary starting with a boozy late lunch at *Rules* in Covent Garden, a few pints in the East End before heading to *York Hall* for an evening of boxing. It just so happened he had a specific event in mind. More drinks would follow the boxing. This was the point at which Grayson planned to join Piers and the men, and introduce them to Joel, fresh off a win. It was the first time he wanted to involve Joel in his investigation. Apply the pressure and get them talking.

The more he learnt about the men though, the more he felt that they were not capable of murder. They wouldn't be able to throw a living person in front of a car and watch as the impact ended their life. He did, however, question if, sitting there in their office, their decadent castle of privilege, perhaps they could have given an order for any inconveniences to be dealt with.

Henry Sloane was the youngest of the three and least senior. A *LinkedIn* page that reflected his millennial propensity for self-branding and promotion.

His public school and university years were interwoven with no less than half-a-dozen summer internships, all at recognised blue-chip companies. Self-important embellishments of job roles described such as document collation and communications management, rather than photocopy monkey and coffee boy. They revealed a character eager to climb the corporate ladder. Post-graduation he spent three years at one of the big banks, before jumping ship to the Black Spear Group to take up a somewhat hollow title of Vice President of Acquisitions. Yes, very on-brand. Limited social media was public. His *Facebook* page, mostly private, had not been updated for a couple of years. Only a few old picture tags of Sloane standing with swimwear-clad friends, raising a glass or bottle, on or near yachts, in places such as Marbella and St Tropez.

The second man in the team was a mystery. Chris Cooper had no social media. No corporate footprint. If it wasn't for the photo on the company website he may have struggled to believe he existed. He had asked Piers about him, but he was none the wiser. Sloane had never mentioned him.

The head of the team, the man who had stood to confront Kamsi at the meeting was of most interest to Grayson. His internet footprint was light, limited to corporate mentions, staged hand-shake photos and panel-speaker appearances. There was minimal information to be gleaned about his background, corporate, education or personal. Late forty's early fifties. A generation or two too early for social media. Although small in stature, he was athletic. A runner, or more likely a spandex-wearing cyclist. A timeline of corporate photos that Grayson had found, illustrated an early greying. Skin tone that was once gaunt and haggard because of long office hours, now embedded with a permanent tan that gave his face a leather-like quality. One that alluded to the fact he now spent less and less time behind the desk and more time in the South of France. A different approach would be needed for further research of Marc Peterson.

♠

He had not been able to gather much information on Black Spear's Head of Acquisitions, outside of his corporate track record, so Grayson decided to take a much more traditional approach. He waited outside of the Black Spear office for Peterson, with the intent to tail him for a while, learn a little more about his personal life, his habits and perhaps even his vices.

To his disappointment, his tail was short-lived, as shortly after 8pm Peterson emerged from his office and walked only a short distance to the *Punch Bowl* on Farm Street. There he gathered with a handful of colleagues to shoot-the-shit about the markets and other opportunities, or 'plays' as they called them.

Grayson bought a pint of lager and a packet of crisps. He found a small table within earshot of the group. He placed his pint on the table alongside the crisp bag now split open in plate like fashion. He retrieved his phone from his pocket and inserted his earphones. He then set a *Youtube* video running keeping the volume silent. He sat back, nursed his beer and listened in.

After a couple of pints, the conversation amongst the men devolved into a pissing contest related to second homes and vacation destinations, both ski and sun of course. From there, to assert the workplace hierarchy, Peterson gave one junior a dressing down. Firstly towards the work hours he kept.

'Seven till seven', he scoffed. 'Part-timer'.

Next, he berated his attire.

'Below par, border-line uncouth.' He said, raising a hand to halt the retort from the junior, before launching into a monologue to the group.

'Appearance is everything in this game. From the way one dresses, to the way one conducts business. If nothing else, remember this. The appearance of a smooth deal, is just as important as the reality of one.'

He pinched at the lapel of one of his disciples.

'Saville Row. All too cliché now. Full of ludicrous art galleries and brash offices for 'hedgy' type companies. Far below our stature gentlemen. God forbid, they have even converted one of the Grade II listed buildings into some American clothes store for pubescent adolescents. All being lured in by bikini-clad young women and topless young lads. Those perfumes and fragrances they wear, aggressive. Downright horrific. See gentlemen the location of one's tailor is key. Saville Row is dead, but Jermyn Street still holds a shred of class, even if some of the older shirt makers have moved down market. In fact, I have a fitting with my tailor booked tomorrow morning at 10am. Unlike some of you kids, I'll be five hours into my working day by then.'

It was at this point Grayson decided that being measured head-to-toe for a nine hundred pound suit would allow him to observe Marc Peterson closer.

♠

He had never owned, or needed to own a suit before. It crossed his mind as he slid the black half-Windsor up to nestle in the sharp white collar. The knot itself he had learnt to tie overnight after studying a *YouTube* video. He didn't like what the suit represented, but as he looked at the mirror he couldn't help but think it fitted him well and that Kamsi would be proud of the effort.

The suit should have fit him well for the price he paid for it. Although he had needed a suit for the funeral, he hadn't expected to purchase it on Jermyn Street. He could have picked up a less expensive one off-the-peg over on Regent Street, or cheaper still on Oxford Street, but given the opportunity presented to him, the money seemed irrelevant.

Especially given the windfall he had recently come into, sat in a safety deposit box just over the road from the tailors.

Unfortunately the opportunity to learn a little more about Marc Peterson, up close and personal, had yielded few results. The tailor appointments had over lapped, but Peterson had been taken into a smaller more exclusive room, out of the sight of Grayson, scuppering his ability to learn anything more about the man. He needed more time with him, Grayson concluded. Especially if he was to determine if he needed a deal so badly and with with such urgency, that he would kill for it.

26 SUITED

As the small gathering departed the graveside, Grayson offered an accompanying arm to Ama and walked her along the pathway, back to the three-car procession waiting in the gravel parking area at the main gate. Ama was doing her best to compose herself after the sombre service. Using an aqua green lace handkerchief she wiped the tears from her cheeks and reflected on Pastor Okereke's sermon. She recited it to both herself and Grayson in a bid to understand her grief as penance towards God's plan and the supposed greater good.

Pastor Okereke had a slight build, tightly shaped jet black hair and a manicured goatee with a light peppering of grey. He looked much younger than his sixty year age. The curled edges of his mouth betrayed a humour, even in the most serious of times such as the ceremony he had performed that morning. His wide eyes, although muddying, invoked engagement.

He garnered a huge respect among the Nigerian community. Always presented in a simple dark suit, pristine white or blue shirt, block tie and mirror shined shoes. Never one to speak ill of others, but made it clear he didn't go in for all of the flamboyant mass gatherings now rife across London. He taught 'that by small and simple things are great things brought to pass.' He was genuinely shocked by the size of some congregations, citing examples where as many as five hundred people crammed into cinemas, warehouses and even bingo halls. He preferred his much smaller assembly, one that included Ama and until recently Kamsi.

Grayson had a huge amount of respect for the man. Incredibly involved in Ama's life since Kamsi's death, he had been not only a shoulder with which to grieve, but helped her with the funeral arrangements. Since the authorities at the *Tower Hamlets Council* declared there was no more burial space in their Borough, he had worked hard to procure a place in nearby Plaistow, at the *East London Cemetery*.

Grayson was doing his best to give Ama his full and compassionate attention, but distracted, he continuously turned his head towards the adjacent path, where he monitored three figures who followed a short distance behind.

Seeing Ama and Grayson approach, the driver of the black sedan at the front of the procession, jumped out and opened a rear door. Ama handed her handbag to Grayson, before carefully climbing into the seat. Once settled Grayson handed back Ama her bag, which she placed on her lap. As he skirted the car to the other side, he called out to Talisa, who was walking towards the second car, with two older ladies from the estate.

'Talisa,' as she approached, he opened the door, 'would

you mind riding back with Ama? I have a quick issue to sort out.'

Purposefully light, as if he had to circle back to the Pastor to donate, or pick up some paperwork, or something insignificant like that.

'Ok, sure dear.'

She peered into the car and exchanged soft smiles with her friend. Once Talisa was settled, with one arm on the door and the other on the roof Grayson leaned forward into the car.

'Ams, I'll see you back at the Community Centre. I'll be right behind you.'

He reassured her, closing the door softly, but with purpose.

As the car drove out of the gate, Grayson turned back towards the graveyard. A scowl crossed his face as rage began to boil. He quickened to a march as he started back up the adjacent path.

Ahead of the others, like an eager sentinel, Lloyd Blake sniggered as Grayson paced towards them. Grayson neither acknowledged him or broke stride as he firmly brushed past, focus fixed purely on the man a few steps behind. Dave Squelch.

In reaction to the aggression, Ryan Walsh stepped between the men, giving Squelch enough time to retrieve the *Colt .45* from his pocket and draw it towards Grayson.

'You turn up here!' Looking down to the gun. 'What you going to do with that?' Grayson hissed dismissively. 'Shooting me aint getting you any money back, you dumb prick!'

'No, but it might cheer me up a little.' Squelch said.

Grayson took another pace towards Squelch. Inches away, he locked eyes.

With an intense stare, he moved his head forward, pressing it against the barrel of the gun.

'See,' Blake exclaimed, 'I told you he's fucking nuts! He's

lost the plot!'

'You think I fucking care anymore! Go on, do it!'

A beat passed. He slowly retracted his forehead from the gun, tilting his head back letting the barrel slide down his nose to an open mouth. Again leaning forward he clasped the barrel with his teeth.

'He's fucking lost the plot, the crazy cunt!' Blake was giddy with excitement.

'Go on. Do it!' Grayson grimaced. The words muffled by the gun.

Walsh stood frozen. Grayson continued to lock eyes with Squelch. Intensity between the two men slowed the passing seconds. Squelch continued to snarl at Grayson, finger on the trigger. As he did so Grayson noted the subtlest flicker of the eye, a small tell escaped Squelch's glare. Moments later, he jolted the gun forward, before retracting it with an audible grunt of frustration.

The forward movement caught Grayson by surprise, chipping a front tooth and splitting his lip. He recoiled bringing his cupped hand up to catch the blood.

With the gun now pointed at Grayson's chest, Squelch began to verbalise his thoughts.

'You are going to give me that money.'

'How so?' Blood spat he fired back.

'You are going to go to wherever you've hid it and get it for me.'

Grayson scoffed.

'The money isn't there anymore. I have invested it.'

'Invested it! Smarmy prick. Invested it in what?'

'A small wager.'

'What kind of wager? For what? With who?'

'Why are you interested?'

'Because that's my money you prick.'

'Correction, fifty K of it was yours before you forfeited it by trying to rob me.'

Grayson had thought long and hard about his options. He knew Squelch would come after him, Blake had confirmed as much. And whilst turning up at Kamsi's funeral had been an unexpected move, to get him off his back, Grayson had a proposition ready for Squelch. He now needed to deliver it effectively, as there was no room for negotiation.

'I'll make nice,' he said, 'I'll pretend that you didn't try and rob me and make good on the fifty K second place winnings. I'll even throw in a further ten grand for the effort, but in return I want something.'

'You want something, do you? What is it you want?'

'I want you to politely fuck off. It's that, or you can shoot me in the head now, receive no money and do ten to fifteen years for your trouble.'

Squelch took a moment to consider the proposal.

'When do I get the cash?'

'Next week.'

'Why next week?'

'Because as I said, it's tied up at the moment.'

'Next week, sixty K.'

Squelch, along with Blake and Walsh pushed past Grayson and carried on down the path. As they disappeared out of sight, the adrenaline subsided. His arms fell to his knees, slumped in exhaustion as he tried to steady his breathing in the damp cold air. The graveyard was now silent, but he didn't feel alone.

'You thought I wouldn't find out?' Joel emerged from a line of trees and gravestones, a hostile tone to his voice.

Grayson turned his head with attention as he recovered to an upright position.

'You thought I wouldn't find out? He repeated, whilst with two hands he shoved Grayson backwards. Stunned, he didn't respond.

'You ran it without me!'

A second shove sent Grayson backwards off of the path onto the grass.

'You've got it wrong.' Grayson asserted.

'All these years. That's the respect I get? You, go behind my back. Out on your own.'

A third shove sent him to the ground.

'You need to focus on the fight. You don't need all this shit. Not now,' he pleaded, 'your whole career has led to this. This is it! I didn't want you distracted.'

'Nah, Brah,' Joel stood over him shaking his head in disappointed resignation, 'guess at some point, we all have to do things on our own.'

He turned and walked away, down the path.

Too stunned to follow, Grayson sat there on the wet grass, trying to comprehend the events.

27 FULL HOUSE

6 JANUARY 2017

It would be about this time that Piers would be leading his guests to their seats. No doubt wide-eyed and buzzing with excitement. Grayson knew that the evening ahead represented a great opportunity for Piers. He was happy, if not delighted to go along with the plan. Well what little of it Grayson had disclosed to him anyway. The invite sent out on Piers' behalf had given him access. His seniors never approved expenses to be speculated on what they believed to be an unobtainable client. Especially if not personally involved in the depravity. They had also grown weary of Piers using the company credit card to pay for dinners and drinks with Henry Sloane, his old school acquaintance. In their view, given Sloane's rank on the corporate ladder, his expenditure had not, and would not amount to any business.

Piers had informed Grayson that he would prove his partners wrong. Single handedly he would entertain the whole real estate team of the Black Spear Group, one of the largest Private Equity firms in the market. One that was actively buying into his patch, the East End, 'Fringe London'.

Piers was surprised to hear that Grayson was covering all of the costs, but having dressed it up as a thank you for the holdall swap, he graciously accepted. Or in his words, 'Fantastic old boy, but I have to say, Tessa did more thanking than you ever could.'

Grayson had given him a wad of cash and *carte blanche* to spend it to show the Black Spear team a good time. He had arranged for a car, restaurant reservation and event tickets. He had told him very little else, other than he would make an appearance later in the evening. He hoped they would be suitably pissed when he did.

He knew Piers was enjoying the moment. He had sent him a text saying as much, that lunch had gone splendidly, the guests were relaxed and he had even had a moment to pitch them some ideas.

For Piers it would be a dream to represent them on just one of their multi-million-pound deals. Such an instruction would launch his career, if not pave the way to early retirement. He would show his father once and for all, he didn't need his money. He would forge his own path.

Grayson was initially surprised that the Black Spear team had accepted the invitation with such vigour. Then again, it was an all-expenses paid night out in the neighbourhood in which they were just about to launch a massive deal. For them it was an experience, the opportunity to 'rough it' with the locals in *York Hall*.

The energy was palpable. With a full slate of fights well underway and two local fighters caught up in a high-intensity bout, the crowd was raucous. For many of the spectators, it was their first outing of the new year, after the customary family break for Christmas.

Grayson assumed that Piers and company would no doubt be a little apprehensive as they edged their way to their front-row balcony seats. They would be met with scowls as they squeezed past the less than gracious knees of a few salt-of-the-earth type locals, most of whom looked like they had as much experience in the ring as out of it. Though, from their prime viewing position, perched perfectly above the ring, they would be close enough to inhale the musty lineament soaked air and feel the heat radiating from the fighters.

Grayson pictured Piers stumping up the courage to offer a solution to the anxiety, pulling his signature gold plated cigarette holder from his jacket pocket. Opening the top and pouring its white contents on to the case. Using a credit card he would set up a few lines and along with a rolled note offer the coke to his three guests.

It would be about this time that Stan would pay them a visit. Stan was a monster of a man. Grayson could picture the scene where a paranoid Piers nervously craned his head to comprehend the sheer bulk of the man looming over him. He imagined Piers offering a sheepish attempt at humour, saying something like 'Could I interest you in a bump?'

Frozen in his offer, like a biblical statue, Piers would be none the wiser as to the reason for the Goliath to be stood in the aisle next to him.

Grayson sent Stan up there to see if they wished to place a wager. He assumed they would ask the odds and instructed Stan to give them a fight program.

He could see it now. Piers would take the program, flick it open. His jaw would drop.

28 ALL IN

6 January 2017

From a damp small windowless room, lit by a single hanging bulb, he released a guttural roar as he worked the punch mitts in a final flurry.

Rowan Quinn watched on, shouting instructions, increasing in volume to a crescendo of commands. Quinn was direct. More than that; he was coarse and affronting. 'No time for time wasters,' that was how he put it. His mantra. And with hundreds of lads, each with their own problems, walking through the doors of *Repton Boxing Club* each year, that was how he had to be. It was fair enough; he did not have time to mentor them all. As a result, he selected and trained only those dedicated to their craft, who excelled and who showed that intangible spark. The same spark that the fighter in front of him showed within hours of his first session.

The second, older but less senior trainer in the room was called Swiss. Not known by any other name, neither inside nor outside of boxing circles. The name had stuck from the moment they gave him it in the late 80s. Very few knew the name his mother had given him.

Swiss, a short stocky man with a flat cap, pierced ear and tattooed knuckles, held open a green silk robe for him. He slid his gloved hands through the sleeves and lifted it on to his back with the hood over his head, exposing 'Repton' emblazoned in gold lettering. Along with the club's name, on his shoulders he carried his ambition and his livelihood. What weighed heaviest was Ama's last words as he left her flat two hours earlier, before he took the short walk to York Hall.

'We are so proud of you. She is with the Lord and is looking down on you. She is so proud. Do it for Kamsi, but most of all, do it for yourself.'

He locked eyes with Quinn, short grey hair with deep-set swollen features. It was the same look given to him when Ama and Kamsi had dragged him to the club all those years earlier. Hope towards completing the hard work ahead. No exchange of words, only adrenaline fuelled growls. Acknowledgement that he was ready. Legs stretched, biceps and pecks now primed, he rolled his neck as Swiss dug his thumbs in to his trapezius muscles to remove any mounting tension.

As the referee walked past the changing room door giving the 10-minute call, the trainers filed out, swinging the door ajar. The room fell quiet. The thick Victorian walls muffled rumblings from the hall above. He sat on a low bench, back to the wall and lowered his hooded head into his gloved hands in a moment of solitary reflection.

He concentrated on the task at hand. Visualised how the

fight would proceed. Running through instructions.

'Find your range. Take your time. Breathe. Work the space in the ring. Maintain your balance and rhythm. Build the combinations. Jab-jab-cross. Breathe. Jab-straight-jab-jab-hook. Breathe.'

Against his cheeks he scratched the course tape that bound his gloves to his wrists. Applying pressure for greater affliction. He replayed Ama's words over and over, each time they cut deeper and deeper with remorse. How had it come to this? He had fought so hard, for so many years. He finally had his shot and now he had to throw it away.

Deep in torment, his head still buried between his gloves, he didn't look up, but felt him enter the room.

As he stood to equal the figure who stood motionless in front of him, he caught his reflection in the mirror.

'You ready?' Grayson said.

'What the fuck do you care?'

'What the fuck do I care?' Anger swelling at the insinuation.

'Want to know why I went it alone? I saw you in St James's. How long did you have that money? Two, three hours?! Straight down the pisser. You couldn't wait to leave and get down there! Sitting there playing stupidly aggressive hands. You didn't have it. You knew it, but rather than man-up and walk away, you carried on and on, until it was all gone. What a fucking waste!'

There was no response.

'And you stand there asking what the fuck do I care? I did it for us. Me and you. Kamsi and Ama. I did it for us.' Grayson now felt the stronger and more dominant.

A snarl misted the mirror.

'You did it for Kamsi did you? You did it for Kamsi?!' Muscles flexed. Now eye-to-eye.

'Look. You know Kamsi's death had nothing to do with the

game.'

'Nothing to do with the game? Why was Squelch at the cemetery then?'

'I had to use the false safe door. Squelch had me at gun point, he thinks he's owed.'

He equalled his tone.

'Look, that doesn't matter. It wasn't them. They didn't kill Kamsi'

'But it was someone? You said as much at the bar. You sure?'

'Yeah, it was someone.' Grayson pictured the men sitting with Piers on the balcony.

'Fuck!'

'You had the money,' a shake of the head in defeated resignation, 'all this time you had the money.'

'What do you mean?'

'It doesn't matter now, anyway. It's over.'

'What's over?'

'The fight. It's done.'

'What do you mean, done?'

'It's done. I have to throw the fight. I'm going down.'

Grayson's head spun, a moment passed as he struggled to comprehend the alternate plans of his closest friend.

'You... you...' he stuttered, he knew before he said it. Deep down he always knew what his friend would say, before he said it.

'I owe. I thought it was the only way to pay. I have to loose the fight. I'm going down.'

'Owe, how can you owe? To who? How much?'

Grayson's pulse raced, he tried to manage the stress.

'Sixty, plus the vig, so seventy thousand. Some Ukrainian guy at St James's.'

As realisation set in, Grayson's breathing became sharp and audible. The night in the casino. He didn't stop. Having emptied his account. He carried on and took on debt.

'I told him I wouldn't throw it. Told him he could place the money on me for the win. I said I'll guarantee it. But he wasn't having any of it.' His head fell, face now buried in his gloves as he growled in frustration.

'Assurances. That's what he said he wanted. I kept telling him I wouldn't throw the fight. And… and…'

He struggled to conclude the thought, but his head had now caught up.

'You don't think this guy would have….?' He tailed off.

'But I told him. I told him I would go down. I would lose. I told him before…'

A shared look of panic. Was this the reason Kamsi had been killed?

Grayson began first to compose himself.

'Look, first thing. You go out there and win.'

'No, I've got to throw it. To pay the debt.'

'No! Just win the fight! You've got to win, because I've placed all one-hundred and fifty K on you winning at 1-to-3 odds.'

Just as they used to test and race each other through odds and values, they concluded simultaneously. Movement and thoughts in lock-step.

'Two-hundred K total.'

Grayson nodded and continued.

'Sixty needs to go to Squelch. To get that prick off our backs,' he paused momentarily as he computed the next part of the equation.

'The Ukrainian will have 2-to-1 odds. To cover the seventy-five owed he'll have to have laid twenty-five. So one hundred will have to go back to him.'

'Ten went to Piers for the entertainment.'

'So that will be thirty left.'

'Right back where we started.'

Anxiety fell as he concluded the calculation.

'Not quite,' he said, 'next up you'll be fighting for the title.'

With the 5 minute call, the referee poked his head into the changing room.

'Alright son? Ready? ...Who you talking to?'

29 GUT SHOT

Mouthing the count as he ascended the twelve stairs from the basement changing rooms to the ground floor. 'Thirteen' said out loud to round off a superstition that had seen him unbeaten in eighteen fights at *York Hall*. Empowered, this was his domain, his backyard.

He reconvened with his trainers, a look from Quinn reaffirming what he already knew. All his hard work had come down to this. This is your shot. You'd better take it.

Energy pulsed against the thick black curtain hung from temporary rigging. Beyond lay an opportunity that moments ago he had abandoned. Stripped by consequences of his indiscretions, but now it was again tangible. It was now up to him and him alone.

Flashing lights pierced the curtain edges. Artificial smoke

seeped in. Base reverberated from the speakers into the corridor in which he stood. Muscles flexed tight as the beats ricocheted off of the walls.

Heart rate rising with anticipation, he closed his eyes to focus and steady his breathing. The music dropped to silence, his opponent now in the ring.

Top billing on the fight card. The last fight of the night.

Sound replaced with crowd expectancy.

In unison, his eyes opened as the curtain parted.

From din to clamour, a synthesised note drew him into the darkness. A resonated pitch rose and fell, rose and fell again. A stressed industrial sound of apprehension.

Suddenly, adrenaline coursed through his body as the laser lights flashed, bass pumped and the lyrics dropped:

I'm sick and tired of running, I'm sick and tired of fronting
  I just wanna be myself, I'm sick and tired of stunting
  I'm sick of strangers in my life, From girl to girl I'm jumping
  Don't know what I'm living for no more but I wanna die for
something

Pacing to the ring, his shoulders bounced and rolled to the beat. Head bowed, his peripheral vision blinkered under the hood of his robe, eyes focused at middle distance. As if taken over by the beat, he threw a short repertoire of jabs as he mounted the stairs to the ring.

I work my ass off, nothing given on a silver platter
  I get more money, then I blow it like it doesn't matter

He angled his tall physique between the parted second and third ropes and sprung into the ring. Feeling the eyes of his opponent on him, he pulled back his shoulders as he paced his corner, exaggerating the two-inch height advantage. His confidence peaking, it felt like closer to four, maybe even five inches.

Vision tunnelled, his mind clear of distraction. He didn't notice the music fade, nor the announcer declare the corner designations, the colours the fighters wore, or their impressive fighting records.

He knew very little of his opponent, Jake Ward and his record of 14-2. Younger, perhaps twenty-five, he hailed from up north, Teesside, or somewhere close. He was well-conditioned, but more bulk than ripped muscle. Quinn had informed him that Ward had strong stamina and looking at his pale skin complexion, that stamina must have developed from training all daylight hours indoors. None of that mattered. All that mattered was the ten three-minute rounds ahead and executing his strategy. Stay long, maintain the distance, work high and take the shots. The referee called them in and the bell rung.

From the opening exchanges, his confidence grew. The first three rounds went well, as he dominated his opponent. Mid way through the forth, he sensed the Northerner's focus fading, his eyes glazing in exhaustion.

A glance to his mentors in the corner, seeking confirmation that his pacing for this stage in the fight was correct, that he was on-track and that the shots he was selecting were precise. To their liking. The acknowledgement and encouragement was there, along with a waved signal from Quinn telling him the time was right to go hunting. To seek an opening and release the combination punches he excelled in, the combination that had finished off the last of his three fights.

Biting down on his mouth-guard he moved in, scoping around, maintaining his distance, as he looked for the tell. There it was. A subtle lowering of his opponents left shoulder, a sign he would throw a right.

Instinct kicked in. A feint left brought his opponents guard up. Overcompensating in the shift from attack to defence, the guard went a fraction too high, obscuring his opponent's vision. A right drop-step at a 45-degree angle took him in close. From here he would make his signature move.

Typically, a fighter would use the drop-step to load the right leg and with a solid footing, look to follow with a high left hook, or throw the right cross. He didn't take this approach. Instead, at the same time he made the drop-step, he would throw a low trailing left hook into the body of his opponent. The shot style was unorthodox. For a split second he opened himself up both high and low, with no defence, but he had an uncanny ability to generate power from such a short ranging shot. And could throw the punch at such a high speed his opponents had no time to react.

In his last three fights, the strike winded his opponents and opened the door to finish them. A flurry of efficient, powerful striking to the unguarded parts of the body and head. His opponents went down, and stayed down.

His timing was perfect, perhaps too perfect. As he faked the left and stepped in, Ward lurched forward. At the last moment changed his intended right jab into a high guard, which opened up the entire right side of his body. The shot landed with a ferocious force, above the belt line into the underside of Ward's rib cage.

The shot was so well timed that Ward immediately dropped a knee to the canvas. A saving grace for Ward, as it halted the chance of the follow-up flurry which would have inevitably ended the fight.

Ward took six or seven seconds to regain his feet. The referee concluded a mandatory eight-count whilst wiping his gloves and checking the resistance in his arms to confirm he could continue.

After he saw his opponent's knee touch the canvas, he

turned to check-in with his corner. Swiss caught up in the emotion, shouting at him, expelling energy on a par with the fighters themselves.

'Finish him off!'

Quinn was calm, mouthing a set of simple instructions.

'Rocking-horse, 15 seconds'.

On receipt of the directives, a grin born of confidence crossed his face. He mused at the entertainment he still got from the reference. Albie Stoker, a Cut-Man for over sixty years, spent most of his years leant over the ropes at *Repton*. Albie got his joy in life doing two things. The first was to pass on crap advice to the so-called 'Upstarts'. Youngsters that came through the club. His favourite piece being, 'keep things bloody simple.' The second thing he liked to do was mix metaphors for comical amusement. It was Albie that gave Swiss his name, something about him being as useless as a Swiss teapot, or a chocolate lighthouse.

'When you're that quick and that powerful, just hit him. Left-jab, right cross. It's not fucking rocking-horse science.'

From that point, in Repton, the simple combination of left-jab, right cross was called rocking-horse science, or to keep things bloody simple, rocking-horse.

He was feeling strong. He knew he possessed the hand-speed to land the right. And, even if the guard come up, he had the power to punch through it. It was now a case of positive intent and getting the shots in before the bell rung to signify the end of the round.

The referee called the fighters into continue.

As he turned back to his opponent, he caught a glance of a figure that he recognised. A man had stepped out of the dark crowd and approached the ring.

At the sight of this man he shuddered. His concentration broke as anxious voices crowded his head.

A beat passed, it was too late to start the rocking-horse

combination, so he pulled up a two-handed guard.

Ward stepped in and threw a series of body shots, striking his abs.

As he curled in, his elbows parted, a strong jab split his defence, catching him square on the mouth, splitting his lip, opening up an existing cut. As he rocked backwards from the shot, the bell rang.

He dropped the gum shield to the bottom of his mouth and tasted the metallic fresh blood as he ran his tongue over his stained front teeth. Staggering to his corner, eyes fixed on the man that had emerged from the darkness and stumbled towards ringside.

30 UNDER DOG

THE RING AT YORK HALL, BETHNAL GREEN, E2

6 JANUARY 2017

'Get him out of here.'

Frantically he pointed his gloved hands at the man, as he returned to his corner.

Composure lost.

He dropped to the small metal stool that Swiss had swung into the corner of the ring.

He spat into the bucket and again gasped the appeal to his trainers as water squirted from a bottle into his face. It choked him as it diluted the blood that streamed from his lip.

His vision was wide, but with no focus.

Chants of the exhilarated crowd broke in and out with a high-pitched whir. It didn't matter he was the local. They'd come to see a fight, they wanted blood and now they had it.

Distracted, he turned his head to search for the man

approaching ringside, only for Quinn to grip hold of his cheeks and drag his head back.

'Control yourself!' He growled. 'Look at me! Focus!'

His eyes tracked as he tried to follow Quinn's command.

Quinn leaned forward and pressed his forehead against his.

'It's ok. It was only one shot. Focus. You've still got this!'

A grimaced nod was all he could muster. He pressed hard back against Quin and snarled. Determination, as he tried to overcome panic.

The bell sounded.

Breathing still heavy, his heart rate had barely reduced.

'Look for your combinations. Maintain your...'

Not registering, Quinn's instructions faded.

He stood and moved to meet his opponent in the centre of the ring.

He shouted back over his shoulder towards his trainers 'Just get him out of here! Get him away from me!'

Unsure, he moved forward, his spring-step stuttered to a stumble. A thousand eyes on him. They taunted him from the darkness of the hall. Jeered him from the balcony.

Off balance he threw a long jab to keep his opponent at bay. He regained some bounce and moved left to right, but did not engage.

Ward, the smaller of the two men, searched for a chance to get in closer.

As Ward approached, he put out another right. More of a fend than a punch. With a little space created, his attention shot back to the man who was now at ring side hitting his clenched fist down on the apron. Shouting at him. Indecipherable.

In anguish, he tried to fight on. The voices in his head swirled, distant pleas from the voice of his friend.

As his focus swung back to the fight, Ward stepped in with

a left hook. Too late with his guard, the shot was firm and connected with his temple, sending his head jolting to the left.

A fog set in. Another shot struck him a fraction above his eye-line. His head rocketed backwards, followed by his step. His vision was dissociated from the fighter in front of him, replaced by a flash of images. A reel of memories brought forward from the recesses of his mind.

As the taxi pulls to an abrupt stop at the top end of St James's Street, he slides a ten pound note through to the driver and doesn't wait for change. A determined stride carries him up the stairs and through the heavy doors. It wasn't over.

As he crosses the lobby he sees Debora. Not right now he urges, as he is drawn into the ballroom. She arrives at his side and clasps his wrist, her look was of concern. Her eyes fixed to his. Her lips move, but in silence.

He shakes free and turns to pace across the guilt edged expanse, shudders as he passes the sofa and enters the smoke filled room. He skirts through the darkness and stops in front of a suited man with a thick wave of grey hair sat at the low lit table. Double or nothing?' He demands. After a beat, the man looks up and addresses him with a chortle, rests his cigar on top of his whisky glass, draws his gold watch free from his cuff to register the time. 'Back so soon?' He says in a foreboding Slavic tone, 'ok, another thirty thousand, as you wish. Double or nothing.'

The roar of the crowd brought him out of the vision. In the front row he sees the grey shot of hair. Shevchuk's affirming nod broadens to a smirk.

Ward lunged towards him. He parries a jab and counters with a left of his own. It lands, then another. He steps forward and forces his opponent to recede. He circled Ward and glanced to his corner where Quinn and Swiss were shouting instructions towards two security guard pacing down towards the man at ringside, who now grabbed at the bottom rope and hollered slurred words into the ring.

The fighters again converged. Both swung right hooks, toe-to-toe, each maintained a left guard, but both made firm connections. Sweat flew from contorted faces. A ring in his head, sounds like an alarm.

Iridescent blue, the digital clock reads 08:15. Heavy headed he reaches across the bed. He find's its empty. Slow to remember, she had left earlier that morning. Relief sets in, but with it regret that she was there in the first place. His conscious jolts as thoughts engage. He has a title fight to train for, but is far too exhausted from the night before. The game, the gun, the safe, the celebration, the girl, Kamsi. One-by-one the recollections hit him. Too much to process on such a hangover.

He has to pull himself out of bed and get a training session in. He needs drive, he needs motivation.

Anxiety runs high, he stares at the wall at the foot of the bed, the shadows move in the gloom. Anger swells, his body is unwilling to move, but he has to train. With a surge, he raises his hand and from a high height drops it, slapping an open palm across his face.

'Look at you bruv. You're a fucking mess.' He screams at himself, as he again slaps his face in a vain effort to wake. 'Fuck. Seriously! I'm in fucking pieces here.' He mutters, as exhaustion kicks in and he collapses back to the pillow in frustration.

He backed away from Ward, and saw that the security guards had moved in closer to their target. With no comprehension of how deep into the round he was, he looked towards his corner for help. Preoccupied, Quinn and Swiss continued to shout at the security guards. Ward was on the prowl, with increased intensity he threw four rapid punches. Legs tired, he absorbed the blows, until a jab broke his guard.

He works the bag, his shots under the moonlight initially sharp and direct, begin to flail as mentally he slips away from his objective. A disconnected conversation plays out in his head as he begins to hit the bag harder and harder working into a rage. Two voices each carry burden.

From a low tucked position, Ward threw a jab. He closed up and blocked the shot, took a step back and countered, left jab, left jab, right cross. Ward evaded the cross, stepped in with an upper cut. It struck him on the chin and sent his jaw upwards.

The glass is heavy in his hand. The whisky burns, as he reaches for the second. He was no better than him. Like father, like son. Broken will, no end to the pain. The voice of his friend brings him back from dispair. It gives him purpose and a sense of determination as he pours the whisky to the sink.

He moved right, his steps rotated his vision around the ring. Ward hunted him, continually he tested his reach. Down beyond Ward's feet, the first security guard had reached the man and grabbed him by the collar. His eyes flicked urgently back to Ward who had moved close. Too close. The rate of his punches was more than he could endure.

The machine next to him hums, bright fluorescent lights overhead. With a weary comprehension he looks down to the drip inserted into his arm. The nurse at his bed side comes into focus. 'You're not sleeping, barely eating and training too hard…' Her words fade, as his eyes close. He has to get out of there.

The crowd had reached fever pitch. The screams pierced. He was sluggish, but Ward's activity increased. One, two right jabs into his gut. He rocked forward into the blows.

Black blazers scuttle off and turned the corner. Confident, cocky even. He recognises the ginger parasite from the estate, flanked by two larger figures. His nerves swell in anticipation. Aggressive shouts bellow toward him.

'Oi! You fucking mental! Still talking to yourself? What you got there?'

Energy drained, his grip releases as the parasite snatches the bag from his grasp. Rage boils, as Lloyd Blake rifles through the contents. Calm washes over him and smothers the anger, as a voice grows closer until it reaches him in a fog. Fist clenched, he strikes. He snarls down at Blake who quivers on the floor. His right bicep pulses, cocked ready to strike again. The Walsh brothers back off. Blake sobs. He lowers his fist and watches as the blood trickles between his knuckles.

He clenched his fist in his glove. Pressed back against the ropes he took punishment from a series of low punches until he rocked forward and clasped Ward. The referee stepped in and pulled them apart. He knew the man at ringside, he shares his likeness. He resisted the security guards as they attempted to drag him away.

'You've got to stop this!' Anger in Ama's face, dismay in equal measure. Unnerved, confused and upset. Kamsi squats beside him. Her grip is firm, her expression compassionate but pained. 'Grayson, you have got to stop blaming him.' She pleads. 'He is in your imagination. He is not real.'

His guard held high, the punches continued to burst through.

As the three figures leave the churchyard, sickening anxiety replaces a moments relief. He had caused this. Kamsi's death, Ama's suffering. It was all his fault. He had risked everything. Striking himself in anger he stumbles backwards, then again, and again until he falls to the ground.

A flash of Ward's glove as it strikes.

'What the fuck do you care?' A face he knows. The brother he loves. 'I did it for us.' Now face-to-face, in his reflection. 'Me and you. Kamsi and Ama. I did it for us.' The words are out of place, me and you. 'Kamsi's death had nothing to do with the game.' He wills himself to believe it. His conscious pleads for it to be true. 'All this time you had the money. It's done. I'm going down.' His strength and power fades, as his focus become clear and the mirror reveals his reflection.

He stumbled backwards, legs numb, he gasped at a seconds respite from the onslaught of punches. The face of the man he knows all too well. Once his hero. Through gritted determination he swung a left punch at Ward with all his might. It missed. His shoulder turned, his action had exposed him. Inevitability set in.

A stranger he had lost years before. Now equal height, he stood eye-to-eye with his dad. There is no glint in his, no pride, no love, only rage. Instincts sharp. He knows it's coming. He could react, but was determined not to. He wants to feel the pain. The pain that manifested in the look from a man he once admired. His hero, his World. For the briefest moment, as the punch was cocked infront of him, he didn't believe it to be true. The ring bearing fist strikes him below the eye. A deep split of the skin as blood pours.

Off of a loaded left leg Wards' hook landed across his cheek, his gum-shield flew, a jet of blood and sweat followed. Muscles seized as he fell. His shoulder struck and whiplash sent his head back in to the canvas.

The last sight before he faded to black was Niall, his father. He pulled against the ropes as the security guards drag him from ringside. He screamed, as he fought and reached out to him.

PART III

31 RIVER

6 January 2018

Slumped on the changing room bench. Motionless. Grayson's trainers spoke to him in bursts, but his attention was distant. Quinn stood to his front and Swiss sat to his side, yet he was alone. A sole witness. A capacity crowd, packed on all sides of the ring. There had been over a thousand sets of eyes on him, but only he had witnessed his best friend vanish. The source of his strength, his determination and resilience, gone. The boxer exorcised from him.

No one would understand. He struggled to comprehend himself. The recollections had flown fast, weaving through patches of his subconscious, stitching together the narratives of two experiences, one of his own as Grayson Day and one of the alter he hosted as Joel Olakunbi.

Confused as the recollections had played out. Which was

which? Who was who?

Quinn and Swiss were animated, but so distracted, he couldn't determine what they were saying. His thoughts were distant. Consolatory, no doubt that's how they were being, consolatory. 'Don't worry champ,' and 'you'll get him next time,' cliche sayings. Well-hearted, but with no substance.

They may not have known of Joel's existence, but perhaps they too had witnessed his passing. Seen the spark disappear, with it his speed and intuition. They too had lost. They had lost the chance at training a champ. With this loss, at his age, it would be the end of the line. He no longer held the unbeaten cachet required for fighters to open doors and move up the ranks. With Quinn, it had been a journey of over a decade. Years of dedication and commitment to Grayson's cause. Blood, sweat and tears, another cliché. The journey from troubled sixteen-year-old until now. Defeated, an equally troubled twenty-eight-year-old.

Quinn removed Grayson's gloves and held an icepack against his eye. The cold relieved the swelling, but it was the solicitude that most consoled him. He cared. For years Quinn had been his only father figure. He provided an example of hard work, structure and routine. Grayson had taken to it. He had craved the outlet to both endure and release pain. The need for pursuance and grim determination awoke a side of him that could push through exhaustion and excel. That side was personified in Joel.

Grayson now knew that journey was over. Quinn may care for him, but he would soon leave.

Sweat had cooled to a chill. His lip wept and the swelling above his eye throbbed, but he was numb to the pain, non-responsive. Minutes ticked through thirty, then an hour. The hall above had emptied. Punters filed out, thrilled from the shock upset they had seen, excited for the new year of boxing ahead.

There were no more words of consolation. Clichés exhausted. First Quinn, then Swiss, said their final piece and took their leave.

Grayson lifted his head to the changing room mirror, where an hour earlier he had shadow boxed a different man. A superior reflection of himself. From the invincible, he now sat broken.

Fractured by the sight of his dad entering the light at ringside. Drunk, stumbling, oblivious as ever to the damage he left in his wake. From the moment he saw him his strength drained. Scared, weak, in an instant he reverted to the fourteen-year-old boy that stood eye-to-eye with his elder. Struck, cast into dispair. His hero lost for ever.

He touched the scar tissue under his eye as he looked at his reflection in the mirror and cast his mind back to the day his dad struck him. He had urged it to happen. He had needed to know a pain different to the permanent gut wrenching sickness that defined his childhood.

He recalled the final vision he had as he come round on the canvas. It was the day he signed his sponsorship deal. Late morning, as he walked across the Estate, on his way to see Kamsi. Grayson shuddered at the sight of his father, sat on a bench outside the Community Centre, waiting for him.

He had been spotted. He couldn't elude him.

'I heard about the sponsor.'

He stood, unsteady.

A shot of empathy crossed Grayson's bow. He looked gaunt, frail, shorter even, but all he saw was rapacity. He wasn't there out of pride for his son, or to congratulate him. There was no approval, no respect. He was there because he had learned of the sponsorship and wanted money.

Grayson put a towel to his face as he recalled the look in his father's eyes. He recaptured the urge he felt in that moment. To protect himself. To protect Joel. It was Joel's sponsorship. Joel's money. His father had no claim to it.

A realisation had set in. That day his father had looked straight through him. He had not seen his son, he had seen his next bottle of whisky.

That was the trigger, just six weeks earlier. That was what drove him to the casino. Joel, a foil for his addiction. His conscious fight to save him, his determination to save their friendship. That moment with his father had disturbed the symbiotic balance he had created. The friendship of Grayson and Joel. Their co-dependence. Their co-existence.

That moment sent Grayson and Joel on divergent paths, with different objectives. Grayson worked tirelessly to protect his friend. He burdened himself with both guilt and concern, to run the business, the game. He spent vast amounts of energy to build a safety net from addiction. All the time, he knew his friend would one day need it. Joel on the other hand, driven by determination interwoven with pride, trained to capacity. He took every opportunity to drive himself to exhaustion, to pursue greatness, to repay his loved ones for their sacrifice. Rather than facilitate and compliment each other, as they had always done, unconsciously he had split and doubled the physical and emotional demands on his body and mind. And finally, Kamsi's death had brought with it a guilt ridden toll that pushed him to the edge.

Clarity was sharp as he reached the thought's conclusion. He now understood. He had seen his father, in the alter of Joel and it had brought home the reality. He had always been Grayson when in the presence of his father. Weak and abandoned. Joel was his saviour. Joel and Owen had never been face-to-face, and certainly not under such intensity. Walking into York Hall that night, his father had started a reaction. Like a neutron striking the nucleus, he had split the atom. Fission and break down. Joel, permanently split from

Grayson in the stark reality of the source of his dissociated identity.

Now faced with the realisation, traits had fractured. Weaknesses were exposed. He didn't know which was which. Who had been whom? And when? Did Grayson lack empathy? Was that why he hadn't stopped to pick up Kamsi? Had he robbed Joel of his patience? And driven him to make rash decisions, spurred on by his addictive demons? He looked to the mirror for answers, but struggled to recognise the man he saw.

Joel was gone. His alter that had given him strength, given him confidence and, most importantly, had given him company. A friend. The antithesis of isolation.

Lights in the corridor fell dark, the security guards the only other souls in the building. They made their rounds, closed doors and switched off lights. The small dank shower room had no appeal, so Grayson reached for his hooded sweatshirt, swapped his shorts for tracksuit bottoms and laced his trainers.

As he opened his bag to load with his wraps, gloves and kit, it hit him. He had not only lost Joel that evening. He had also lost one hundred and fifty thousand pounds. That money was supposed to resolve their problems and give them a fresh start. It was enough to get both Squelch and Shevchuk off their backs for good. Mind you, the result would surely have satisfied Shevchuk. After all he would have won his bet, thinking Grayson had thrown the fight as instructed. Squelch still posed a problem, but that would have to wait.

He threw his bag over his shoulder, turned off the light and navigated along the corridor toward the exit.

Their problems. Their opportunity. Their fresh start. Grayson would have to come to terms with the fact, there was no longer 'their'. It was just him.

A stranger in a flat he had rented above the nail salon. He placed his bag on the floor and leaned back against the door as the latch clicked shut. Silent. A voice that had always kept him company had vacated his conscious, yet left behind memory. He had known where to find the flat and which keys to open the door. Yet as he stood there in the kitchen, it felt like it was the first time. A visitor.

Cold and soulless. A small bedsit, the lights hung bare, white walls and the minimal furniture consisted a bed, a single chair and a table. A digital clock sat on the side table, it read 02:18. In the corner stood a clothes rack that held only training wear and smarter attire for church. There was no television, no decoration, no photos and no mirrors.

He sat on the edge of the bed and looked at his surroundings. He waited for his friend to arrive. To take form, take action, or to take-over. No-one came.

His eyes closed as soon as he laid back.

He woke with a start. The digital clock read 06:58. Bruised ribs ached as he stood from the bed. Pangs shot to every extremity, but it was the clarity that was most painful. First his mother, then his father. Kamsi and now Joel. He always lost those he loved.

He had to get out of the flat.

His walk carried urgency, he broke into stride, then ran. Only as he emerged onto London Bridge did he realise he had run the same route. Followed the same streets. Following his father's stride. Longing not to be left alone.

The Thames flowed beneath, twilight exposed the water's movement. Staring due east he remembered how Tower ·Bridge and the walled castle had once filled his head with wonder. A six-year-old boy lost in daydream that innocence readily could protect. Castles, dragons, and knights played out vivid quests in his boundless imagination. He could still recall how he believed he could fly, as his father carried him across the street and onto the bridge where he now stood.

He remembered his father placing him down. The jarring of his feet stirred him from his daydream, but made way for a burst of excitement. They had arrived to the 'big' bridge. His father's look of approval filled him with elation. He spun around and ran giddy to the mid-point of the bridge. Joy and freedom as he dodged and weaved amongst the ambling passers-by. And there he was, clasping at the overhead rail with both hands, aligning his head to the gap in the granite wall. That was the spot. The perfect view.

The vision brought a chill that made the hair on the back of his neck stand. He scanned along the bridge until he reached that very spot and visualised his six-year-old self looking down in awe at the HMS Belfast. Kings, queens, knights, castles, and dragons were fun, but nothing compared to the immense battleship that sat on the river below.

The bow stood proud as it pointed up toward him. The grey-green hull shone in the morning light. Turrets and guns were ready for action. His six-year-old imagination was transported aboard the vessel adorned with colourful flags fluttering from the mast. Out to sea, full steam ahead, waves splashing as high as the Captain's deck on which he stood. 'Incoming!' he heard a Crewman shout across the gangway. His head rocked backwards to see two fighter planes swooping in at high speed. Now at the gun turret, he took aim, left arm aloft as he wobbled backward from the granite wall. 'Fire!' He shouted. He got the first one. The sound of the plane diving to the water, audible for passing commuters to hear. Then the second, down it went. This time the crash even more pronounced. His arms raised above his head in glee. A cheer went up. He was the hero. He had saved the ship once more and relished in the glory.

He recalled his view back to his dad how he stood face towards the sun, eyes closed. They had set out on the same adventure every day that summer. A quest towards his mum. The princess trapped in the formidable tower of Guy's hospital.

He had always had a vivid imagination. When happy, it innocently played out in fairytale and battle. Later that same imagination would create Joel, a best friend, an alter, a protector.

Grayson watched the morning light bounce off the water beneath Tower Bridge, seamless to the sky above. He now realised that his father had stood there that day to compose himself, contain his emotions and ready himself for the unimaginable pain ahead.

Released memories. Suppressed, but never forgotten. Exposed by the emptiness. He had always had Joel, Kamsi and Ama to turn to.

He imagined plunging to the water below.

Joel was gone, Kamsi killed. Ama needed him now more than ever.

As dawn broke, he breathed as calm as the river flew beneath him.

He had always be in awe of Ama's strength, her ability to carry on through tragedy. Starting from the day she gathered her younger sister to escape northern Nigeria.

His emptiness filled with resolution. He had to find out why Kamsi had died? And who was responsible? He owed that much to Ama.

32 RAKE

7 January 2018

With no screech of a pre-dawn alarm, he woke naturally for the first time in months. As he rose from the deep slumber, it was the brightness of the room he first registered, and then the utter stillness. He daren't move. He looked up to the ceiling and waited for the silence to break, but it maintained. Not only in the room, but in his head.

He reached to the side table for his phone. Pain shot across his chest, his body ached, but his head was calm. Numerous red dots awaited him, missed calls and messages. Ama and Estella had checked in to see how the fight had gone. Then later sent messages of concern, having heard word of the outcome.

No less than fifteen messages from Piers. Shock at Grayson being in the main event on the fight card, followed by photos of the fight from the balcony. A series of group selfies during the fight, in which he and his guests had pints in-hand and eyes wired. Later messages of consolidation, followed by pinned locations of their post-fight movements. Finally a message that resigned to the assumption that Grayson would not join them.

A message from Shevchuk, brief and to the point, simply read 'Good Boy!'

A voicemail from Squelch might have raised concern, but he deleted it unheard and made his way to the shower. Water hot enough to flush his pale skin. The high pressure soothed as it struck his shoulders and a sense of ease stuck with him as he considered his next steps. His mind clear. There was a void, but with it a determination. A clarity of purpose, that he would fill that void with answers.

As he dressed, he reviewed the wall, analysed the notes, maps and photographs. He didn't trust Blake and Walsh for a moment, but he had faith in his interpretation of Blake's reaction. They had witnessed Kamsi fall out into the road, but it was the before and after that was of most importance. Before she carried three or four weaved bags, he had seen that himself. And after, they were gone. He had re-watched the dash-cam footage from the taxi over and over. There were no bags on the street as the taxi approached and she was not holding them when she fell. Therefore they must have been carried round the corner, and taken the opposite way up Mowlem Street. He had checked for CCTV. There were cameras installed on the side of the *Bestway* building, but none of them faced the corner.

He panned across to a photo of the TX4 taxi and Greenwood. He had witnessed his testimony to his peers in Piccolo's. It was a sombre and honest account, but why had he run? The question tormented him. The police had determined he had not been drinking and was driving within the speed limit. That fact was shown on the dash cam. His reaction and braking given the conditions were not under question. He called the ambulance and must have stood up to questioning when the police arrived. Everything pointed to the conclusion the police report reached. An accident. Grayson was convinced otherwise.

Grayson stepped into the bathroom to clean his teeth. As he reached to open the cabinet door he caught his gaze in the mirror and shuddered. A subconscious reaction, but the trigger was identifiable. It was lucidity, a clarity he hadn't previously experienced.

He tried to get at an idea held deep in the recesses of his mind and darted back into the kitchen. His finger immediately located the photos of Greenwood and his family. He voiced his thought process in an attempt to cling to it and not lose it.

'New taxi,' his finger slid across the photos.

'There. The "little red bus." That's what they called it.'

'Musher…Musher… Musher.' He searched for the comment from one of Greenwood's Daughters.

There it was. The one mentioning the family holiday in Tenerife.

'The old man can't wait to take it back to black.'

Back to black. That was it. He had identified the lucid thought.

The taxi had been restored to black, but not all the way.

He grunted in frustration as he cast his mind back. His memory not working at the desired speed.

'Livery. A new one. New signage…'

He closed his eyes and took his mind's eye back to Greenwood's drive. The moment as he approached the taxi.

The slogan read something about 'reshaping the East End'.

The logo. A series of buildings formed of arrows. Or, points.

It clicked.

'Point Developments. That's it!'

He kicked away the chair and swung open the MacBook that sat on the table. Opened a new tab in the browser and typed in Point Developments.

The first search prompted was a UK website address, the remainder were foreign. He clicked on it to reveal a holding page. No website, yet the domain had been purchased.

In a moments deflation he stepped back. Took a breath and then surged again. He opened up the Companies House page and fired in a search for Point Developments. Nothing.

If he was so keen to get 'back to black', why did Greenwood need the new livery?

Something about it didn't sit right.

And most importantly, why did he run?

'I guess there is only one way to find out.'

It was as he finished the sentence when the unease set-in, as he realised that he spoke out loud.

33 TELL

He had watched Kim Greenwood leave the house ten minutes earlier. There had been no sign of the daughters all morning.

This was the moment. He set off with purpose, passed the taxi sat in the driveway. Quickened past the bay window and shot a look into the lounge. Mike Greenwood was sat, feet raised on the recliner section of a beige sofa.

The melodic tune of the doorbell ended just as Greenwood entered the hall and reached for the door. Muttering to himself as he swung it open.

He gasped.

As he went to slam the door shut Grayson beat him to it and wedged his foot in the gap. He dropped his shoulder into the door. The thrust sent Greenwood stumbling backwards.

In panic, he darted into the kitchen.

Grayson followed. As he entered, Greenwood drew a large knife from a block.

Grayson's advance halted.

'Look. I just want to talk.'

Greenwood continued to back away. The knife trembled. A frail old man, it was clear that although armed, Greenwood did not consider himself in ascendancy.

With considered steps Grayson closed the space, guiding Greenwood to the back corner of the room.

'I just want to talk.' He reasserted, palms now up in good faith.

'The livery', he continued, not entirely sure where his question was leading.

'Why do you still have it? And who are Point Developments?'

Overcome with panic Greenwood did not comprehend. He continued to back away, now skirting the kitchen countertop.

'I've not said a word. Please!'

Greenwood was now boxed in, at any moment his flight might turn to fight. Grayson had to act quick.

He lunged forward throwing both hands towards the knife.

At the last second he slipped inside and caught Greenwood by the wrist, driving it into the countertop. The grip released and the knife fell to the floor, out of reach of both men.

In immediate defeat Greenwood slumped. His back slid down the cabinet.

Grayson retracted. A moment passed as both men gasped for air.

'Now,' he said ensuring he had Greenwood's full attention, 'I am not here to hurt you. I simply need to ask you some questions.'

'Point Developments...' he paused. 'Wait.' His brow narrowed.

'What do you mean you haven't said a word? Said a word about what? To who?'

Greenwood cowered even smaller.

Clearly perplexed, it took an age for him to stumble to an answer.

'The Police... Look I don't want any trouble.' His voice inflected in plea as he continued, 'I haven't told them anything. It's not my business. Please. I have a family.'

Empathy and exhaustion calmed Grayson.

Greenwood was clearly scared, but there was something there. Through fear, he was holding back on information. Grayson needed to extract it.

'Look!'

'For the final time. I have not come here to hurt you. If I wanted to, don't you think I would have already?'

A shade of relief passed over Greenwood as he considered the question.

'But why are you here? Why were you in the cafe? And why are you following me?'

Grayson wanted to get straight to what it was Greenwood was holding back on, but his instinct told him to trade some information to get there.

'Ok, ok.'

He took a moment to breathe and compose himself.

'Kamsi Olakumbi was my auntie.'

Greenwood looked on dubious.

'Look, ok. Not my actual auntie. Let's say she was a close friend. She raised me.'

A small nod of understanding encouraged him to continue.

'I don't believe she fell. I was at the cafe because I wanted to find out more. That's why I listened in and that's why I followed you. I just wanted to ask you some more questions.'

Greenwood eyes conveyed he was beginning too comprehend.

'Now. Why did you run?' Grayson said in a tone that invited an answer.

'Initially. I thought you were collecting.'

Picking up on Grayson's look of confusion, Greenwood continued.

'I owed some money. I borrowed a few grand for the house extension. The bank wanted a whole bunch of paperwork, so I went to see a guy. It was supposed to be a short term thing. See? The livery money was due in.'

The information did not flow as freely as Grayson wished, but he focused on maintaining patience.

'But the developer went bust and didn't pay me. The residents stopped their project. Protests or petitions or something.'

Grayson's gestured for Greenwood to get to the point.

'Then there was the accident. After, I wasn't driving. I wasn't earning, so I missed a couple of payments.'

Greenwood was showing his age as he meandered through the explanation.

'I thought you were collecting.'

'What convinced you otherwise?'

'The guy told me he hadn't sent anyone. I went straight to him. See? Well, I stopped off and borrowed the cash from a mate, but then went and paid him.'

'As I say, I didn't want any trouble, it was only supposed to be a short-term loan. So I thought you were col...'

He froze mid-sentence. A revived wave of panic set in as his eyes widened.

'Wait. How do you know where I live?' Now clearly Greenwood's mind was in overdrive.

'Your daughter's social media. Look, don't worry about that.' Grayson shot back. 'Tell me what you meant, when you said you haven't told the police?' He struggled to mask his frustration.

'You! You smashed my taxi. Stole my dash cam.' Greenwood said, now in complete panic.

'You stole the dash-cam. You thought it was evidence. It was you!'

Greenwood kicked his legs towards Grayson, then attempted to stand

'Why are you doing this?' He yelped.

'Doing what?' Grayson said as he reached out, grabbed Greenwood by the shin and reeled him in.

'Coming here, like this?'

Grayson pinned Greenwood, who for all his worth couldn't muster much resistance.

'Because my Auntie was killed and I need to know what it is you're not telling me. What you're not telling the Police.'

Grayson clenched his fist and held it high.

'I've tried my hardest to do this the nice way. Don't force me, Ok?'

Greenwood quivered under his mass.

'For Christ's sake. Just tell me!'

'Alright, alright.'

'I saw someone. There. That night. After the accident.'

'More.' Grayson demanded.

'There was someone there. On the corner. Just standing there in the rain.'

'What did he look like?'

'It was too heavy. The rain I mean. With the taxi lights as well. I couldn't see him. I couldn't see properly, but he just stood there.'

'Just stood there?'

'Yeah. I called the ambulance. When I looked back up, he was gone.'

Grayson released his grip on Greenwood.

'Why didn't you tell the Police?'

Greenwood was calming.

'I don't know. Look. The way she fell. I didn't want any trouble.'

'What do you mean?'

'The way she fell. It was too sudden. He must have pushed her.'

Grayson sat up. His back struck the cabinet. The reveal from Greenwood had taken the breath from his lungs. He peered down to the knife, now in reach.

Greenwood caught his eyes, in panic.

Grayson reached and grasped the knife. Then slid it away across the tiled floor.

A wash of relief passed over Greenwood.

The dash cam footage was engrained into Grayson's memory. He considered it in light of what Greenwood had told him. It took only a second to capture the moment. Until this point when looking around and fixing his sight down Mowlem Road, Grayson had assumed that Greenwood was looking for a street sign. In reality he was looking at the assailant. His clarity now frustrated him. Greenwood was an old school London taxi driver. He had taken the *knowledge* and been driving the streets for years. He would have known exactly where he was and the name of the roads. Christ, the proof was right there in his recollection he gave in Piccolos Cafe.

'But why not tell the police?'

'I wanted to, but then.' He paused to retrace his rationale. 'I just made a decision. I have a family. I didn't want to get involved in other people's business, you know?'

'I don't know,' Grayson said in resignation 'She has a family too,' his tone fell with exhaustion 'She had a family.'

'I was going to go to the police after you followed me from Piccolo's, but I got home to see the taxi smashed. I thought it was a message. So I didn't'

Grayson said nothing, just shook his head in resignation.

'I'm sorry.' Greenwood said.

Grayson nodded in acknowledgement.

'At least tell me, what did he look like? What was he wearing?'

'I really couldn't see. I was in shock and the rain was so heavy.'

The look of Greenwood was now one of compassion. It was clear he wanted to give him something.

'He was about your height. I couldn't see much more.'

34   CHECK-RAISE

8 JANUARY 2018

He carried a brand of smug self-importance. Dressed in chinos, boat shoes and a pink striped shirt tucked into a navy round-neck sweater. Uniformity that had all the flair of a corporate logo. A padded gilete jacket completing the hedge-fund-chic ensemble. Chris Cooper had broad shoulders, and seemed to have put on a few pounds onto a once athletic frame. A frame that was of similar height to Grayson.

Cooper was on a conference call and wanted everyone to know it. Earbuds in, yet holding his phone close to his mouth, he paraded around the patrons outside of the *Guinea Pub*. His facial expressions put on a show as if he wanted to scream from the rooftops, 'I'm very important. It's New York on the line. I'm working so late because it's very important.'

Having missed out on the opportunity to drop in on the

evening he had sponsored, Grayson had wanted to get back on the trail of The Black Spear Group. Today his focus was on the number two in the team, Chris Cooper. Grayson had been observing Cooper for only minutes, before he stepped outside to dial-in to the conference call. Fortunately for Grayson's cover, no matter the cold temperature, there was always a dozen or so men stood in the small lane outside of the pub. The necessity to smoke whilst enjoying a pint.

He had to stay out of sight. Cooper would surely recognise him following the fight. Fortunately for Grayson, he seem too wrapped up in himself to notice anyone else around. Even when he pitched up against the pub wall just three or four yards away. It was as if the weight of Cooper's insecurity was too much to wade around. Grayson listened in and tried to piece together the context of the call. Something about the man didn't sit right. Intense and over eager. He nodded and chewed on each statement, as if to prepare his brain for digestion.

Suddenly Cooper perked up. It was his turn to speak. Perhaps an update from London, or something to that effect. Whatever it was, he seemed to get hard at the opportunity to say his bit. Make his valuable contribution to the very important people on the New York call. His enthusiasm even more amplified.

Even with little knowledge of corporate goings-on Grayson determined that other participants on the call had probably tuned out at this point. Pulled their mobile phones from their pockets to skim read some emails, or flick through the latest posts on *Instagram*.

Cooper opened with a cannon of statements. Business jargon Grayson had to concentrate hard to make sense of, if at all. We have a prime position. We can of course facilitate appropriate leverage. The projected returns are strong.

The numbers outside of the pub had dwindled, Grayson

tensed as the odds of him being spotted increased. Those that remained were unfazed by the loudness that Cooper presented with. His mannerisms and reactions where all over the place. Like a stage actor, he jumped between characters in a play. Although he never betrayed his underlying estuary tone, his accent seemed to morph as he pieced together a series of buzzwords and lingo, which Grayson assumed the call participants readily decoded.

'I'll stick the music on and see who dances,' he said in a Dick Van Dyke like accent that seemed to suggest he would try to implement an idea. 'I have limited bandwidth,' rather than jus say he was busy, his tone now back across the pond, very Manhattan. 'So I'll touch base with the legal team.' As if he had been brainwashed by a corporate cult.

Grayson tired. He had learnt very little about Cooper, but as he finished his beer in a sign of resignation, Cooper said something that revived his attention.

'Let's just say on that issue, we have had a touch. A touch of good fortune.'

Now back with an East End stress, Cooper as yet had said nothing explicit, but Grayson had a read on him. He knew exactly what he was talking about. He knew there were life and death stakes to his statement, but had chosen to make light of that fact. To Grayson it was clear that the 'good fortune' he had referred to, was Kamsi having been killed, clearing a potential obstruction from their purchase of the *Cranbrook Estate*.

It took a long time before Cooper confirmed Grayson's intuition. Limited details had been provided to other participants. It was as if the subject of the conference call had changed. By now Cooper asserted what seemed to be a hollow knowledge about urban planning and their legal rights versus obligations of morality. He repeated over and over again similar points at increased volumes until they sounded plausible. Opinion morphed to fact. As if said twenty percent louder would make it actual.

He started statements with phrases such as 'hear me out' and the 'reality of the situation.' His tone was now almost ecstatic. Energetically he exaggerated every beat, a overarching story of run-of-the-mill events told to the rhythm of Gordon Gekko telling Jerry 'if it looks as good on paper that they were in the kill zone. Lock and load.' This went on for five minutes before finally, in response to a question he told Grayson everything he needed to know.

'Local resistance? Well, there are others. The residents are in communication, but have not yet put anything formal together.'

Cooper paused. To receive a follow up question, Grayson assumed.

'One or two. There is a new Community Centre Manager, but not sure she will be effective. The one to watch out for in my opinion is the sister. She was at the meeting and seems to have most of the facts. She also knows everyone on the estate.'

As he listened to Cooper, the context became crystal clear. Anger swelled, his heart raced. He was talking about Ama. He had referred to one of the kindest people he knew as resistance. His fist clenched. He swallowed the urge to confront him. With a bruised and swollen face, he was careful not to make eye contact or draw Cooper's attention, but it needn't have mattered. So distracted, as he put his empty glass to the ledge that hung below the window, he missed. The glass fell to the ground, it smashed to the jovial cheer of three of the punters nearby.

Cooper looked, rolled his eyes at Grayson and continued to round off his piece with an anecdote about his wish to get out to the golf club, if the missus would let him. As he hung up the phone, he looked smug, proud of himself.

Grayson stood in disbelief. Cooper had not recognised him. He surmised that it must purely be down to the different attire, shorts and gloves in the ring. Jeans, jacket and a woolen hat now. That was it, the different attire. It could also be the inordinate amount of beer, wine and coke Cooper had consumed that night, before the fight had even started.

Grayson worked to maintain his composure as his rage boiled. The sensation was odd. It was if the exposure of Joel had drawn new battle lines up on the field of his conscious. There was no longer one voice of reason, in control of one of aggression. His thought was clearer, less misted and more accurate. He had the information he required and knew what to do with it.

35 DRAWING DEAD

9 JANUARY 2018

Work stopped as he walked in. Two men in overalls downed tools to a work bench. Neither broke their stare as they moved round behind him, now covering the doorway. The only way in and out of the rundown industrial unit.

Further into the darkness, a figure squatted, welding two metal rods. The blow torch was extinguished and mask lifted, to reveal the stunned expression of Ryan Walsh. As he moved closer, the expression developed into a sanguine grin. He was keen to see what reaction his boss would have to this visitor.

With his mobile held to his ear, Squelch looked up from the desk, through the internal window to the workshop floor and the silhouetted figure walking towards him. He ended the call and stood from his chair, placing the mobile on his desk.

'You've got a fucking nerve.' Squelch burst out of the small office.

No response.

'They told me you were fucking crazy, but now you are taking the piss, bowling in here.'

Grayson continued forward with a gritted look of determination and stopped two yards in front of Squelch.

'You seem to be empty handed.'

Again, no response.

'Assume it didn't go exactly to plan?' He gestured to Grayson's swollen eye, blood lip and battered face.

'Or did it? A little dicky-bird told me that some Ukrainian fuck made a bundle last night.'

The smell of burnt electric grew stronger as Walsh and the two men at the door moved in closer.

'You don't have it? Do you? Fucking mug!' Almost surprised, Squelch looked deep for an answer. His face now within inches. Nostrils flared as he sniffed for signs of money.

Grayson answered with his silence.

'Prick-fucking-mug!' Squelch said, spit escaping in his rage. His eyes darted to one of the men behind Grayson, who on command swooped in and struck him across the back of the legs with a wrench.

Grayson dropped to his knees. Another strike, this time under the arm into his ribs.

It was enough to send him to the floor, writhing in pain.

Squelch leaned over him.

'Take my money. Blow it. And I find out you were lining the pockets of some fucking Cossack.'

He had no strength to fight back. That part of him was absent.

'I didn't throw anything.' Grayson said as he recovered to his knees.

Squelch squatted in close.

'To be honest, I don't give a fuck if you threw it or not. My fucks are given about my money and the fact you don't fucking have it.'

A boot swung in and kicked him in the chest.

'Wait... Wait. I've got an offer for you.'

'He's got an offer! He's got an offer!' Squelch paraded around Grayson, a circus ringmaster, playing to his audience of three.

'There's always a fucking offer. Well perhaps, sonny-fucking-jim, I'm not interested in your offers any more... Perhaps I'll just do you right now and pop you in the post to your aunties... Oops, I'm sorry.' He leaned with a forced chuckle, 'your aunty.'

The word stung, but he refused to show it. Grimacing at the pain from what he assumed was a broken rib. His lip had re-opened and blood streamed.

It used all of his effort to lift his head and look Squelch in the eye.

'It's 50 K. In a sit-down poker game.'

'Listen here you mug. It's 60 K with the vig and I've got half a mind to make it seventy.'

It was his last shot. It could all end here. He summoned the strength to continue. He wished Joel was there.

'You get your 50K, no vig and you have to sit and play.' Grayson said.

'Sit with who?' Said Squelch now intrigued by the conditions

'Well... Me, one or two others,' a beat passed, 'and a Ukrainian.'

He watched Squelch's reaction for a tell. Had his offer landed?

'How you gonna stake it? Me and you? Yet turn up here light?'

Squelch flicked his eyebrows ordering another blow with the wrench.

'Another one of your hidden bag tricks?'

Shit. He reacted quickly.

'Wait wait... look,' he raised his hand to stop the strike. Then continued, 'Out of the kindness of my heart, I'll sweeten it for you.'

Squelch raised his hand and signalled for his man to pause.

'Sweeten it for me... He's gonna sweeten it for me. Go on then. I'm listening, you greasy little mug.'

Grayson took a moment to compose himself. To ensure he landed the pitch.

'If you win, you win. And we're up straight,' he confirmed Squelch was along for the ride. 'If you lose and I win, I'll make good the 50K plus the 10K vig.' Yes, still engaged. Now for the prickly bit. 'If we both loose, then fuck it, we've lost. We're through.'

Squelch took his time. He paced around chest puffed. Before he returned to Grayson, drew his gun and held it to his face.

Calm washed over him. He didn't care anymore. Without his mother, without Kamsi and now without Joel, maybe it just didn't matter. He had made his peace with Ama. Estella would find happiness elsewhere. It may be a blessing if Squelch ended it for him, right there on the damp workshop floor.

'You're gonna give me my money even if you win. You really are a crazy cunt... but you know what. I've heard your offer and quite fucking frankly I don't agree the terms.'

Grayson held his breath and braced.

'So here it is. Best and final. Get it while the going's good.'

Squelch ran the gun down either side of his face, metal cold against his ears and cheeks.

'Not only had this better be legit... but even if I lose, even if you lose... You are still gonna pay me that money.'

He prodded Grayson in the face with the barrel.

'Cos if you don't it's not just you I'm gonna do. I'm also gonna kill that fat bitch auntie of yours. She'll suffer first though.'

36 NUTS

'At first, we thought he was just an imaginary friend.' Ama placed a cup of tea for him on the side table, removed a throw from the sofa and sat.

'Not so uncommon you know. For a six-year-old. I had one as well, when I was about that age. Her name was Chichi. We would sit and read together. And practice our music.'

A small smile broke the edge of her lips as she transitioned from one happy memory to the next.

'Then Kamsi came along, and I forgot all about Chichi.' A soft smile gave way to a sniffle at the emotion of her lost sister. She composed herself and continued.

'You had such an active imagination back then. You would come into the hospital, every day with a new story about the dragons or castles. Or planes and battles-ships.'

Grayson held his tea and warmed his hands. The walk over although brisk had been chilly. The memories Ama described were fresh in his mind, as only days before he had stood in the exact spot on *London Bridge* looking down at the *HMS Belfast. A*nd eastwards towards the *Tower of London* and *Tower Bridge.* He had tried to comprehend how a simple fairytale imagination had evolved into the creation of a person and further still into a dissociated identity, one which he had carried for over twenty years. As he drank his tea Ama helped him join the dots.

'You were upset, your father couldn't help you,' Ama continued, 'but you were peaceful, positively distracted by your friend. You would hide away in your bedroom playing cards for hours and challenging yourself with different games. Remember the clock game? You were safe and content. We thought that was the most important.'

Grayson considered what Ama had told him. She had not told him anything he didn't already know. Yet at the same time the information was new. As if locked away deep in the recesses of his mind and only now the key presented.

'Have you always known?' He said.

'Well, at first it was not a problem. I mean yes, you were quiet and withdrawn, but you seemed ok. You kept Joel hidden, but we always knew he was there. It only started to be a problem when you got older. When you started to blame him for things. Small things at first. Remember? He spent all of your pocket money at once. Or you were late up for dinner, because Joel wouldn't leave the playground. Do you remember?'

The question was genuine. Acknowledgement crossed his face.

He immediately knew what she meant, but still had to process it. He had experienced the events through the lens of two identities. Grayson or Joel, sometimes both, sometimes in conversation with each other. He recalled that he didn't want pocket money, he knew Joel would spend it. So if he didn't get the money in the first place, he could control Joel's urges. Then he remembered being stood on the playground, looking up at the flat window, he knew Ama and Kamsi could see him, yet the game was fun and Joel would not give him back the ball so he could go home.

'It was getting worse. We were scared, you know? There would be weeks where we wouldn't see you. You would be in your room for days. Niall... well your father I mean. He was never there. You were on your own.'

He recalled his room on Old Ford Road. He remembered the times his father would stumble in and out of the house. Or was passed out on the sofa. Or the time he smashed the television with a bottle, for no particular reason.

'When your father was about, it seemed to get worse. Rather than just a friend, you had two different behaviours. Not bad, just well... I mean you both, Joel and Grayson started to speak differently. Sorry it's hard to describe.'

Grayson reached out for her hand and urged her to continue.

'The words you used, even the accent. From that point it was clearer for us to tell which identity you were using.'

'And then... when he hit you.' She froze, as she realised she may have been too blunt. 'Well, when that happened we were scared for you. We were scared that Niall might hurt you again. He was always drinking, and you, well you had grown to the same size and had become angry. You blamed Joel, which made it worse.'

'Kamsi wanted you to see a doctor, but I said you would be ok, if we could just get you away from your father, so that was when you moved in. Remember?'

He did. Each and every last detail, perhaps too much. Like a 3D movie without glasses, there were two memories of the events, but only when distant did they marry up. Up close, it was as if he had two separate experiences.

'It all calmed down. You were happy. Your school reports were improving. Especially maths and PE. Until the fight with that Lloyd Blake.' Her detest of Blake was clear.

'I saw it.' Grayson said, 'I saw how it was.' He began to grasp at the thought. 'I remember Joel coming into the alley. He punched Lloyd. He saved me.... but.'

Ama interjected.

'That's what you told the teachers. That was the problem for them. Me and Kamsi understood, we love you... but they... well they had no choice, you know? You wouldn't take responsibility, no matter who's fault the whole thing was.'

'But then I saw it!' An urgency to his voice, 'That's what I'm trying to say. The other night in the ring, I remembered how it actually was. It wasn't Joel. It was me. Only me.'

Ama nodded her head in acknowledgement.

'It's always only been you. All of your strengths, all the weaknesses. It's only you.'

Grayson caught himself as he consolidated the weaknesses. The lies, the addiction. Even the smallest of deficiencies led to the worst outcomes. He played that moment over and over, as he passed Kamsi in the taxi. He wondered if in the moment Joel had appeared, but he knew the truth. It etched the horror of the moment into his memory. Hard coded on Grayson's conscious.

'Kamsi was still worried. We both were. That fight spoilt your education and you came away with no grades. We were both just so upset. She wanted to take you to the hospital, but I knew they didn't deal with that stuff back then. And we couldn't afford any other help. We argued. She wanted me to stop acknowledging Joel, but I couldn't. I always told her you had him under control. I think I ended up loving him as well… But perhaps she was right.'

Her compassion was hard to look at. The burden she carried for him, someone that was never her responsibility. Grayson again reached to her hand. If he could be only half as kind as this woman, he would be proud.

'Then Linda Blake came into the Community Centre, screaming and balling about how you had broken her son's jaw. She was drunk of course, but she showed me and Kamsi a photo of his face.'

Although her eyes had welled, she broke into gentle laughter.

'That was when Kamsi said we should take you to the boxing club. It seemed like the perfect compromise.'

As Ama joined the dots, Grayson began to identify the picture, as she continued. He had more questions, but bit his lip. Everything that Ama had said make perfect sense, he didn't wish to jolt her from this explanation. He poured them both a second cup of tea as she continued.

'The boxing was great for you. It seemed to bring everything under control. A regular pattern.'

She could read him, she knew what he wanted to ask. Perhaps he had picked up his intuitive skills from her.

'Yes,' a slow nod of the head. 'You switched to Joel the moment you walked into the boxing club and switched right back the moment you left, except on Sunday. Joel would come to Mass. Kamsi would joke that Joel was your religion, six times a week and twice on Sundays.'

She sighed.

'On the most part, he gave you balance, but that's the thing. It become normal. For years. With the help of Joel, you were doing well. You were focused, determined. There were things that you credited to him, but well…' with a smile of resignation, 'you were happy.'

He stood, deep breaths as he took it all in. Ama was now in

full flow.

'Even when you moved up West, we thought it was fine, maybe even a positive change, you know? You would be further away. Less chance of bumping into your father. I wanted him out of your life for good. Kamsi disagreed. You are the only thing we ever argued over, you know?'

She smiled as she brought a handkerchief to her eye.

'She said I had got my way pretending Joel existed. And so she would keep your father updated, if he promised to leave you alone.'

Grayson shook his head.

'You know he came to the fight?'

Revelation on Ama's face developed into comprehension of what Grayson was about to tell her.

'Right in the middle of the fight he came stumbling up to ringside.'

He recalled the pressure. The moment when his exterior veneer shattered.

'That's when it happened. It was as if it all unravelled.'

Ama understood.

A moment passed as they both reprocessed.

'You know it's different now?' He said.

'I know. I see it. You are different as well. You should know that. Your soul is at ease.'

He perched on the edge of the sofa next to her. They both reached for their cups of tea.

'Grayson, you have lost nothing. Now you see it, his flaws can no longer hold you back. If you want to do something else, you can. If you want to carry on boxing, you can, but as you, as yourself. All the strength he possessed is within you. You don't need to rely on him anymore. It's time to say goodbye.'

He knew she was right. It was a lot to comprehend.

'It's time to move on. You should find a nice girl. What

about Estella? She was lovely. Do you still see her?'

Ama could read him. Joel would always talk him out of relationships. Especially Estella, who he long cared for. Grayson had once thought Joel was protective, or jealous of the time he spent with her. He now realised that it was the part of him that didn't wish to expose Joel to Estella that had held him back. Ever since his mother passed he had feared the loss of someone he loved so much. And now with Kamsi, he realised, he had no control over loss.

He pictured Estella, her wide smile. The abundance of energy exaggerated by her blond curls. Most of all her eyes. The way she looked at him. She knew his flaws, she understood his pain and loved his joy. He knew he had to tell her. Explain, rather than fight it.

Ama reached across and clasped his hand with hers.

'Maybe it's time for us both to take this opportunity and move on.' She searched for his acknowledgement. 'Kamsi is with the Lord, there is nothing we can do. And although I miss her every moment of every day, I know we'll be together again.'

In that moment, as he thought of the love that Ama possessed both for him and Kamsi, he realised that the opportunity to love was greater than the pain of the loss.

At the same time it reminded him of the questions that surrounded Kamsi's death.

'But the bags?' he appealed, 'I need to find out who was involved. Someone was there when she died. Someone is responsible for Kamsi's death.'

Ama opened her arms and brought him in for a hug. As she released she held his shoulders, making sure he met her eyes before she continued.

'It would be my wish that you stop this. God has his reasons. And we must move on.'

His acknowledgement and agreement was met with deep

breaths of relief.

'Ok, I can stop, if that is what you want. I can stop. I just need one last favour.'

37 EQUITY

SHAMPERS, KINGLY STREET, SOHO, W1

12 JANUARY 2018

Grayson edged between white-clothed tables adorned with French dishes and red wines. He weaved between busy waiters and waitresses and found the small steep staircase down to the private dining area.

Piers, a self-described bloody good egg, had made his first call to his new acquaintances at the Black Spear Group. He informed them that due to the terribly unforeseen circumstances, namely Grayson being knocked-out, the man himself hadn't been able to join them as planned. He had therefore requested their company at a boozy Friday lunch. Initially, they had not shown interest, Henry Sloane had called Piers to give him a heads-up that only he would be there. On Grayson's instruction, Piers had told Henry to inform his seniors that the subject of the lunch would be the

Cranbrook Estate. That had got their attention.

His second call had been to his father's friend, who happened to be the proprietor of a quaint restaurant nearby. Its doors open for almost thirty years, *Shampers* was the kind of place that is always full, but could usually squeeze you in. On the *Carnaby Estate* the weekends were busy, as one of London's prime retail destinations, just a stones throw from Regent Street. During weekdays it played host to casual business lunches as office dwellers strolled in from Soho and Mayfair. It was a business meeting of a sort that Grayson envisaged, but one to keep off the books and outside of their decadent Mayfair office.

The three men came down the stairs into the room. A low green gloss ceiling, brightly up-lit and a red tiled floor, the walls overflowed with local artwork of varying sizes and quality. Grayson and Piers stood to greet them before they settled at a central table.

'Gentlemen,' Grayson said, 'I ordered some red wine and medium cooked steaks all round.'

There was a general nod of approval from the group, so he continued.

'Sorry for not joining you the other night. Things didn't go quite to plan.' He gestured to his swollen eye.

'Anyway, I hope you had a better night than I did.'

He was not one for niceties, but given the situation and his intensions, he adapted.

He was aware of Peterson's eyes as they scanned him up and down. Amused by the light hearted introduction, but reserved.

Cooper was the first to respond.

'We all lost a few quid backing you, but Piers more than made up for it with the hospitality.'

Piers had informed Grayson that post fight entertainment had gone 'swimmingly'. They had ventured to some late night bars in the East End before they headed West. They had spent the last of the cash in a Gentlemen's establishment in Holborn.

The waiter arrived and poured the wine, which he had opened to breathe before the three men had arrived. As he departed, two waitresses emerged from the kitchen. They set down the steaks along with thick-cut chips, side-salads and a selection of sauces.

Grayson was eager to get to the point, but knew the form and that he would be better served to let them eat their meal, drink a glass or two, before he began what he hoped to be a fruitful interrogation. He didn't have much of an appetite, but to save face and to bide time worked through his steak.

As the group rounded off their last mouthfuls, the waiter emerged and took an order of four espressos. A typical procession where one member of the group placed an order, and the rest jolted into action, reversed their position and took one as well. Grayson declined, now focused, he wanted to begin the conversation at the appropriate tone.

'Gentlemen.' He addressed the group, but directed his attention to Peterson, the senior member.

'Thank you for your time. I wanted to speak with you about you buying the *Cranbrook Estate*.'

Peterson shot a look a Cooper who in turn, shot a glare towards Sloane. Shit rolls downhill. Their involvement with *Tower Hamlets Council* and the *Cranbrook Estate* was clearly something they wished to keep well under wraps. Peterson, perturbed, responded for the group.

'I am afraid that is not something we are pursuing at present.'

Grayson expected a denial. To his credit Piers had prepped him well. One of the first notes he had was that they would deny, deny, deny, all the way until the ink was dry. At which point it would be press release and self-promotion galore.

'Ok,' Grayson responded with a tone of acknowledgement. The game had begun.

'You know there has been a rumour of a sale? And the tenants of the estate know?'

'We hear a hundred-and-one rumours a day across our markets, most of which do not materialise.' Peterson said.

'In essence, everything is for sale. If the price is right.' Cooper piled on.

'But you know of the rumour about the *Cranbrook Estate* specifically?'

'As I say, everything is for…'

'Yeah, yeah. Everything is for sale. If the price is right.'

Tension grew as Grayson concluded Cooper's statement.

'I get it, but let's say you are looking to buy the *Estate*…'

Peterson, agitated, stood to leave.

'Piers, thank you for Friday evening. Good fun all round.' He put his coat on and shook Piers' hand. 'Grayson, I wish you the best in your career, but I'm not sure what you are looking to gain from us here and quite frankly I have to get back and clear my desk for the weekend.' He offered Grayson a hand. He took it and answered.

'The reason I asked you here, is I would like to know how far you will go to get a deal done?'

He released his hand and observed him. There was no discernible reaction. Grayson considered he may not have understood the context of his question.

'As I say. We are not specifically looking at that project. Well,' he paused. 'Well. Thank you again for the lunch.' He turned towards the stairs and hesitated. 'In fact. Sloane, be a lad and pick up the bill and I'll see you back at the office.'

Grayson couldn't let him leave.

'In mid-December my auntie, Kamsiyonna Olakunbi, was killed.' Grayson announced.

Peterson stopped and returned to the table, as Grayson

continued.

'I understand you were acquainted. Or should I say had confronted her at the *Cranbrook Community Centre*.'

He studied Peterson who retook his seat. Initially taken aback, he swiftly regained his composure. Grayson was forming his read. With both focus and use of his peripheral vision he picked up on every tell the three men were giving up. As he would do at the poker table, he put them through his mental lie-detector. Easing of the shoulders, dilation of the pupils, movement in their chairs. Every action and reaction informed him, gave him a small piece of the puzzle and now, with the men in front of him, he was starting to see the picture form.

'Well firstly. There was no confrontation. We simply raised objections to the manner in which she was informing the residents. All speculation and no real concept of how things work.'

He caught himself and steered away from the patronising tone to one of sincerity.

'Terrible accident. I am dreadfully sorry for your loss.'

Those words, 'sorry for your loss', they were reactionary but scripted. Yet, what else were you supposed to say to someone you had just met? As Grayson weighed the sentiment, Cooper broke the silence.

'Yeah, terrible. Listen I hate to point out the obvious, but you said that she was your auntie yeah? She is black. And you are... well... not.'

Grayson ignored Cooper and instead pushed the agenda.

'It wasn't an accident. She was killed.'

They met the statement with muted shock. It was clearly not something the men had expected to hear this Friday lunch time, whilst they digested their steak. The reaction was genuine. More pieces of the picture landed.

A moment passed, Piers cowered away as Peterson and

Cooper glared at him. The look was transparent. You have brought us here for this?

Peterson folded and placed his napkin on the table with purpose.

'I'm sorry. You have brought us here because?... because you think we would have something to do with that?... Well sorry to disappoint you, but we were no doubt just as shocked as you to hear the tragic news.'

'The *Cranbrook* play was one of many in London that crossed our desk. We chose to participate in the meeting to get fully appraised of the situation on the ground. I mean no offence, but that doesn't mean your auntie was not wrong in her interpretation of the facts.'

Sloane sat silent, Cooper was less tactile.

'Pretty insulting this! You bringing us here to cast aspersions.'

Grayson had formed his read on the men. The picture was complete. He was not looking at those responsible for Kamsi's death. Frustrating, but it was a determination he was prepared for, one that he accepted, especially in light of his promise to Ama to drop the investigation.

They may not be Kamsi's killers, but that didn't mean he couldn't continue with his plan.

'That's not the reason I asked you here,' he said to reengage them.

'It is my understanding that, not only do you plan to buy the *Estate*, but the process is quite far along. And that the only thing that could derail it, would be a substantial protest from the residents.'

Both Peterson and Cooper prepared to retort and repeat their earlier assertions, but Grayson rose his hand to pause them.

'Look, hypothetically, let's say my information is correct. You plan to buy the Estate and any activity of the Residents would be "resistance"…' He specifically directed the terminology towards Cooper to assert his knowledge of the facts overheard at the *Guinea Pub*.

'Let's just say I could have a significant influence whether that resistance continues, or whether it just well… disappears.'

'Disappears. Who do you think you are? Dynamo?' Sloane jested, with an underlying tone of arrogance.

'He's a Magician Marc.' He clarified to his senior colleague, clearly confused to the reference.

'There is however a small catch.'

'Go on.' Peterson said,

'My magic trick will cost you one-hundred grand.'

The figure evoked little reaction from the men. Cooper feigned confusion, but Grayson registered the sustained concentration of Peterson.

'As I understand it, the kind of pricing on the *Estate* is over one-hundred million. So 100 K would be a drop in the ocean,' palms now open, 'what's that? Two weeks of lawyers fees. Or the cost for some dickhead agent, no offence Piers, to write some bull-shit market report.'

'Hypothetically speaking. What makes you think we would need your magic?' Peterson said,

'You might not need it, but I believe it would make your life a hell of a lot easier to take it. You know,' a pause for effect 'The appearance of a smooth deal, is just as important as the reality of one.'

Grayson detected that in Peterson he had struck a chord. The catch was hooked, he now had to reel him in.

'Kamsi meant a lot to the community. People are upset, no one more so that her sister, my Auntie Ama.'

At this reference a pained question crossed Cooper's face, but Grayson continued.

'In Kamsi's name she will fight it. She will fight it tooth

and nail.'

Having listened in on Cooper's contribution to the conference call, he knew this was a fear of the men opposite, Cooper had said as much verbatim. Slowly, slowly he worked the reel and drew them ever closer.

'I have known her my entire life. I can tell you her grief will manifest and she will devote her life to stopping that sale.'

'What do you require from us for her and the residents to drop any protest, before it starts?'

'I told you my fee. Yes let's call it that, a fee. Is one-hundred thousand. To be provided in cash within the week.'

In unison Peterson and Cooper let out a forced laugh. Peterson, as the senior took the reigns.

'That's not the way we do business. And even if it was, do you seriously think we could come up with that kind of cash?'

'I don't think. I know you can.'

'Ok, seeing as you like hypotheticals so much. Let's say hypothetically, if that was possible, what assurances could you give us?'

'None. It is simply an opportunity I'm presenting. You guys have to work out if you want to take it. We all know it's a small fry amount for your potential upside on the deal.'

'As I say. Although we know of the project in question and attended the meeting, we are not dialled-in on it.'

Deny, deny, deny.

Taking Petersons lead, Cooper and Sloane stood to leave.

'Before you go. There is just one thing I would like to show you.'

Grayson took his phone from his pocket, flicked open a video. Once he had the attention of the group fixed on the screen, he pressed play.

38 DEAL

The video had worked. The phone call had come through on Thursday morning. He had been expecting it and upon seeing the withheld number, Grayson imagined the voice on the other end to be a deep husky male, so was surprised to hear a higher pitched female voice who without pause gave him a location and a time. Her tone was professional, courteous even, as if suggesting this was like any other business meeting. Perhaps this was, he wasn't to know. Having questioned who would meet him? And how he would be recognised? He was told only that identification would not be an issue.

It was forty-five minutes of waiting at the Japanese Garden in Regent's Park before Henry Sloan arrived, exuding arrogance in the slow pace of his stroll.

He arrived with minimal acknowledgement or form of greeting.

'Here.'

He swung a black rucksack from his shoulder and passed it to Grayson.

'Waste of bloody time if you ask me.'

His voice was drawn, an octave deeper than expected and purposefully accurate.

'I'm really not sure why we are going to such extent at this point. We certainly don't need help from you, or Fitzgerald-Smithe, that Trustafarian Chin. It's just charity if you ask me.'

Grayson wondered if anyone at any time asked Sloane for his opinions, or if he just ended each sentence that way so he could assert them.

'Well, ta.' Grayson said and set off.

As he walked back to his apartment, he contemplated what Sloane had disclosed. The smallest tells, three simple words used nonchalantly, gave away so much more, "at this point." It was clear they were getting close on the deal. Perhaps the Estate was more vulnerable than he thought. Time was ticking.

♠

He decided to walk down to St James's Street, slung the rucksack over a shoulder and set off. To avoid the evening hustle of Regent Street, Grayson cut by *Liberty* and down Kingly Street, past *Shampers* where he had met the Black Spear team a week earlier. The meeting had left Grayson with two conclusions. The first was that eventually the money would come in. He had been confident that the video he had shown them had been persuasive. A recording of Ama saying she would drop any protest organisation against the selling of the *Cranbrook Estate* if they did what Grayson asked of them.

The video made it clear that she didn't know what Grayson would ask, only that she trusted him.

The second conclusion Grayson had reached was that the men had not been responsible for Kamsi's death. Whilst Henry Sloane was on the fast-track to become a well-established arsehole, at the moment he was ineffectual, essentially an errand boy for his senior colleagues. His impression of Marc Peterson was one of arrogance. In the Black Spear firm, it seemed the more arrogance you possessed, the further up the ladder they rose. Or perhaps he had it the wrong way round, and it was the seniority which fostered the arrogance. Either way, observing him at the *Punch Bowl* and in the Jermyn Street tailor, his impression was of a man that valued appearance above all else. Not only in his personal attire, but in the optics of every facet of his life. He had wondered if he would go to any length to ensure his operations run smoothly. He had also been the aggressor at the Community Centre meeting, but face-to-face Grayson convinced himself that he showed genuine empathy. There had been no obvious signs of a coverup. Any mis-truths the group told about their interest in the *Cranbrook Estate* were as transparent as the wine glasses they drank from.

Chris Cooper had been the biggest prick of the bunch. Antagonistic to the core. Keen to scrape his way up the corporate ladder by hook or by crook. At the *Guinea* he had had some choice comments to make regarding Kamsi's death and how advantageous it would be to them avoiding any resistance from the residents. Grayson carried disdain for the man, but like his boss was too readable when face-to-face.

The Black Spear team were not responsible for Kamsi's death and he had made a promise to Ama to drop his investigation and move on. And whilst it killed him to do so, he had every intention of keeping that promise.

39 TABLE STAKES

19 January 2018

As Grayson entered the private room at 50 St James's Street, Squelch lent back on his chair, his navy polo shirt road up with the movement and exposed his gut above his belt. He stubbed out his cigarette into an ash tray and looked him up and down.

'You better not be fucking me around you prick.' He said as he tugged down at the mid-section of his shirt.

'Nice to see you too David.' Grayson retorted, 'Hi Lex.'

Lexi O'Shea gave Grayson a soft smile and continued to count and place chips in to stacks on a side table. It was clear she had been keeping herself to herself, staying as far away from Squelch as possible.

Grayson swung the bag onto the table and unpacked twenty bound wads of cash, each containing five thousand pounds.

'Don't mind, do you?' The question rhetorical. Squelch reached over and flicked through the wads, checking near enough every note.

Just as Squelch concluded his check of the cash, Kabhir entered the room. Smartly dressed, black pleated trousers and long-sleeved black shirt. He handed five thick envelopes to Lexi and took his seat.

Shevchuk was the last to arrive, as if notified the group were ready for him. He strolled in and shot a grin Grayson's way. His face laced with the confidence of a man about to play on house money. Grayson shuddered at the sight of the man as he struggled to recall a distant memory of this very man, in this very room.

Once seated, Lexi placed equal stacks of chips in front of the men and ran through the structure.

'We are starting at 50 - 100. The blinds will raise every twenty minutes and it's winner take all.'

'Questions?' Without pausing for an answer. 'Very well then.' Wasting no time as she split the deck of cards face down on the table and snapped off a shuffle.

As he ran his fingers across the smooth felt to collect his cards, a sense of déjà vu struck. His recollections of the game were patchy, limited to the vignette flashbacks he had experienced in the ring. A reel of a movie from the eyes of his alter, the film was grainy and incomplete.

The edges sharp against his thumb as he peered under the two cards dealt to him. He had to stay alert. The stakes tonight were higher than he had ever played. The cash was one thing, but the threat that Squelch made towards Ama was his main concern. Squelch's patience exhausted. He didn't hide his disdain at being sat in the room, Grayson's read on him was that this time, he would carry out the threat. Tonight would be the last time Grayson would have the opportunity to appease Squelch and get the prick off his back. He didn't want to consider any alternative outcome.

Shevchuk had readily accepted the invite to the game. As far as he knew he had beaten Grayson before at the very table they sat. He was unaware that it was Joel who was dominant that night. It was Joel he had defeated. It was Joel who had lost the thirty thousand retainer money. And it was Joel who an hour or so later marched into the room and demanded double or nothing twice over, eventually loosing a further sixty grand. Seventy, including the vig. With Joel exorcised, it was Grayson who had gone down in the ring. It was Grayson who had unintentionally settled the debt. And now it was Grayson who was determined to win back the money.

The first hands were tentative as the men silently scoped each other out, trading blinds and small wagers.

Over an hour passed before Shevchuk broke the stoney silence abruptly addressing Grayson in his deep Ukrainian accent.

'You are a fighter. I'll give you that.'

Grayson didn't react. He was out of the hand, but had a fix on Khabir, who was considering raising a mid-position that Shevchuk had placed. Khabir paused a fraction too long. If he wanted to bluff, he had missed the opportunity. He knew it, and with a shade of frustration he folded his cards.

'The other night. You had me worried there for a while.' Shevchuk said, not even acknowledging Khabir as he scooped up the chips that Lexi had pushed his way.

'You should know. I was afforded some very good odds.'

He scanned the table from Grayson to Squelch and continued.

'It was as if someone was betting heavily on the other side. Betting on you to win. Tell me one thing. You wouldn't know anything about that, would you?' He said with a knowing chuckle directed at both Grayson and Squelch.

'I won't pretend to understand it, but I knew you would not cross me.' His voice more threatening with every word. He reached for the cross on his gold chain.

'He will punish those who do not know God and do not obey the gospel.'

'Fucking hell!' Squelch piped up.

'Putting on a right song and dance over there? Do they teach you all to speak like that at Gulag school?'

Proud with himself at his dig, Squelch returned his focus to his cards.

Shevchuk sat still, his stare fixed on Squelch. Grayson was relieved at the briefest of moments to be outside the spotlight of either man. His chair felt comfortable and even more so now that he did not have to consider Shevchuk's question. His focus was now on winning this game and ensuring Ama's safety.

For the first time of the night, all four players called the same hand. The flop came out, the three community cards placed on the centre of the table.

Jack (spades), Jack (diamonds), four (clubs)

Squelch, as if buoyed by serotonin produced from his encounter with Shevchuk, piled into the hand and made a large raise. The Ukrainian quickly folded, as did Khabir.

Grayson did everything in his power not to shake his head at Squelch. That was not the way to play, far too aggressive. As much as he despised the man, he needed Squelch to remain relevant in the game for the sake of Ama. Grayson was holding *Jack (clubs), Jack (hearts)*. He had the nuts, four of a kind. An unbeatable hand, but taking that money off of Squelch at this point made no sense. He needed to allow him to stay in the game and increase the chances that the end result would be Ama's safety. That said, he had no confidence in Squelch's ability to beat Shevchuk or Kabhir alone. He exhaled in frustration as he folded his perfect cards. Only to be enraged further as Squelch berated him for falling for his bluff.

'Can't believe you folded that. Pussy.' Squelch laughed.

'Your bluff was fucking obvious,' Grayson expelled. 'It was fucking charity.' He immediately regretted that frustration had got the better of him. Even more so that his play would look weak in the eyes of Shevchuk and Khabir, who were without context.

Squelch got the message. He knew the truth. That Grayson truly saw the bluff and had deliberately mucked a winning hand, but he couldn't help twist the knife.

'You should have fucking called then. Fucking mug.'

Lexi, acknowledging the increased tension, called a five-minute bathroom break. Shevchuk and Kabhir made their way to the door. As they exited, Squelch pushed away from the table, stood and skirted round. As he passed Grayson, he stopped and placed a firm hand on his shoulder.

'I didn't fucking like that,' he said, 'here. Just to be clear we're on the same page, look at this.' Squelch pulled his phone from his pocket. He flicked open a message from Blake sent thirty minutes earlier and played the video.

The video was point-of-view as a gloved hand pushed open a door. The video moved through into the flat beyond and scanned the brightly lit room. All the lights were on, but there was nobody in the lounge or kitchen.

Grayson's shouldered seized. He inhaled sharply, as he realised. It was Ama's flat.

The video continued to pan, coming to rest on the manila bedroom door. The hand pushed open the door to show Ama laying on the bed. They had her gagged, her ankles and wrists bound with gaffa tape. Two figures stood over her, both dressed in black, both wearing balaclavas. The larger of the two held a hunting knife, which he moved towards Ama's throat as the camera zoomed to expose the terror on her face. The video ended.

'Now. Let's not be fucking around, or the boys will finish up with her.' Squelch said as he patted Grayson on the back and exited towards the bathroom.

Grayson slumped, he pinched the bridge of his nose as pain pulsed between his eyes. He had known that Squelch was not bluffing in his threat, but the video had crystallised it. His gut wrenched with anxiety, but he had to push past it.

As the players resumed, the pace of play immediately increased. It was not long into the session when Shevchuk took a large pot and eliminated Kabhir from the game.

It was one less player to compete against, but now the Ukrainian possessed a large chip lead. One which he would surely use to his advantage, if steps were not taken quickly to reduce it. The time was ticking, who would get to Squelch first.

Grayson reached for his cards.

King (spades), King (clubs)

Shevchuk folded, and Squelch raised. Was this the opportunity? Grayson called to see the flop, out came the three community cards.

Six (diamonds), Five (hearts), Two (diamonds),

Squelch aggressive to the core raised. Grayson took time to consider, but with a pair of kings, he called. The turn card was placed on the table. The fourth community card.

Jack (hearts)

Following two checks, Lexi dealt the river card. The fifth community card.

Queen (diamonds)

Upon seeing the diamond, without hesitation Squelch called 'all-in' and pushed all his chips to the centre of the table. Grayson maintained his focus on Squelch. A beat passed, then another, before Squelch broke. The smallest saccade, eyes flicking top-left and back. Grayson caught it, now certain it was a bluff. His shoulders eased. He knew Squelch was representing the flush, but didn't have it. Squelch's jaw tensed. He knew he had given up the tell.

'Oi, mug! Before you go calling. Just you think about it.'

Grayson had thought about it. It carried a huge risk to both he and Ama, but he needed those chips to compete with Shevchuk.

'Call.' He declared and laid his cards on the table.

'Well. You better know what you are doing, boy.' Squelch said. As he dismissively threw his cards face up to the table to reveal his busted flush, just as Grayson suspected. Squelch stood and paced from the table, pulling up a chair on the other side of the room, but certain to maintain Grayson's direct eye line.

Now heads-up with Shevchuk, who was still chip leader and maintained a posture of confidence. One that suggested they had been here before.

Grayson worked hard to control his breathing and heart rate. The money now meant nothing. His sole focus was on Ama. The duress she was under and how quickly he could stop it.

'So here we are again.' Shevchuk declared and took a long draw on his cigar.

'From boy to man. The fighter. Tell me this fighter, why did you take such persuasion to go down? You clearly had debts to pay.'

Grayson tried his hardest to ignore Shevchuk. His attention was beyond his shoulder to Squelch who was now on his mobile phone.

'So much could have been avoided, if you just learned to play within your means.'

'And here you are again. Out of your depth. The money...' he shrugged, 'that may not matter to you, but looking at the man in the corner...' he gestured toward Squelch, 'I would suggest you are in no position to lose today.'

Grayson stayed silent. With every hand dealt, he pictured Ama in pain and kept his focus. He studied Shevchuk at every turn. This time it was different, no longer blinkered by his alter, no longer chasing loses, he saw beyond the Ukrainian's facade; he saw the patterns develop.

After twenty minutes of heads-up play, Grayson spotted an opportunity, as he lured Shevchuk into a large raise, but it wasn't one he would usually play. The risk was too high.

He paused for a moment, his thoughts drifted to Kamsi, his mother and back to Ama. He had always lost those he loved. He couldn't loose Ama.

He couldn't play the hand, it would be too aggressive. Too risky. The sort of hand Joel would have played on instinct alone. He pictured his friend by his side, urging him to play the hand.

He considered Ama's words, "All of your strengths, all the weaknesses. It's only you."

He took a deep breath and slid his chips forward with an 'all-in' re-raise. This was the pot, but nothing pre-flop was certain.

Shevchuk placed his cards face up on the table. A wry smile, acknowledging they were the same cards he had beaten Joel with.

King (spades), 10 (spades)

Grayson turned his cards, calculating a two-thirds chance to win. It wasn't as high as he hoped, but he was committed.

Queen (hearts), Queen (spades)

Lexi leaned forward and dealt the flop. The three cards.

King (clubs), King (hearts), Ten (spade)

Grayson's heart pounded, his head fell as his odds dropped. He had gone from a high chance of winning, to an almost certain chance of loosing the hand, and the game.

A slow shake of Shevchuk's head suggested the cards had been inevitable. Fate even.

Lexi almost apologetic.

Squelch approached the table to get a closer look.

'Wait there boys. Looks like it's ending here.'

He said into the phone, maintaining an intense stare towards Grayson as Lexi dealt the cards.

First the turn.

Queen (diamonds)

Then the river.

Queen (clubs)

It took an age to sink in, before Grayson eventually rocked back in his chair. His hands covered his eyes as he exhaled.

The cards had come through. He had won.

Shevchuk slamed is hand to the table in frustration. The strike instantly calmed his demeanour.

'The righteous person may have many troubles, but the Lord delivers him from them all.' He said.

No doubt further words were said as Shevchuk departed, but Grayson was too caught up in relief to notice. Slowly he gathered himself and made his way across to Lexi who had set out the winnings on the side table. Grayson gathered twelve bound wads and through them into a holdall, which he handed to Squelch.

'There's sixty grand there.' Grayson said.

Squelch immediately turned the cash out onto the table. He muttered as he began inspecting the notes, every other word a curse.

'Satisfied?' Grayson asked, as he watched Squelch put the last wad back into the holdall.

Squelch held his stare at Grayson, finally reaching to his pocket, retrieving his phone and hitting dial.

'Stand down.' He said.

Grayson assumed he was addressing one of the Walsh brothers.

'Lucky for him, the little prick has come through.' He hung up.

'This is the last I want to see of you.' Grayson said, 'and you can tell Blake to walk the other way if every he sees me at *Cranbrook*.'

'We'll see.' Squelch said as he turned to the door, 'in the meantime, don't go getting too big for your boots.'

After giving Lexi five thousand, Grayson packed the one-hundred and thirty-five thousand into the black rucksack and slung it over his shoulder.

40 PRICE

20 JANUARY 2018

'Moving on'. That's how Ama described it. He respected her wish. And now with Squelch paid off and the winnings safely stored, perhaps now they had a chance to move on.

Grayson knew with Joel's disappearance, he wouldn't have the edge in the boxing ring he needed. The loss had closed the doors to the title fight and the sponsorship would soon evaporate. Ama tried to convince him he still possessed all the strength and skill needed, but deep down he didn't want to fight without him.

He missed Joel, but had drawn positives from the clarity he now possessed. Determined to maintain this lucidity. He had been dissociated from himself, dissociated from his father. He had lost the fight, but found himself. He and Ama had decided that he would go to his father to put his issues to bed once and for all.

It was a short walk to the *Arden Estate*; he passed the flat above the nail salon on Roman Road, which he had vacated the week before. He had taken his training gear to the *Salvation Army* on Mare Street and his suit over to Ama's flat. He would still accompany her to Mass each Sunday, but it required a new routine.

He checked his phone for the address, a photo of the note Ama had written for him. The bedsit in which his father lived. He had run through the moment a hundred times. What he planned to say to him. Forgiveness, that's what Ama had convinced him of and he respected her opinion. He needed to forgive him. It was the only way he could truly move on.

A grey overcast morning, he walked through a maze of alleyways and rundown parking garages until he found the row of terraced flats. High walls with 'No Parking' painted in large letters gave way to overgrown trellised fences that protected small unkept ground floor gardens. He navigated round to the front of the row and found the number. The rusted front gate hung open on busted hinges.

A heightened sense of anxiety almost stopped him in his tracks. He half expected Joel to be at his side, giving hime strength in his convictions, but he was absent.

After a few breaths to compose himself he approached the door and knocked. With no answer he tried again, this time heavier. There was no response. He scanned the street. A white transit came to rest on a speed bump, before it signalled and pulled out to the street with a low rev of a diesel engine.

Grayson turned the handle, the latch unlocked, and he pushed open the door.

'Niall,' he called out. Unsure if he had ever addressed him by name. He stepped into the small hallway.

He opened the single door to reveal the entire bedsit. The first thing he noticed was the trash strewn across the patched carpet. Beer cans, home-brand whisky and vodka.

The second thing he saw was Niall sprawled out on the sofa. It was a sight he had not seen in years, but one he recognised. His first instinct was to pull at his arm. It fell heavy as it swung to the ground, striking several empty orange pill bottles.

He shook him by the shoulder.

'Niall.'

There was no response. Harder this time. Still nothing.

He placed the back of his hand by his mouth. He was not breathing. With urgency, he felt for a pulse, but couldn't detect one.

He pulled his phone from his pocket and called 999.

'Ambulance.'

'Help. He's not breathing!'

'He's laying here on the sofa.'

'Alcohol. Pills. He's overdosed.'

The dispatcher asked him for the address. As he recited it, he reactively scanned the small bedsit. That's when he saw them, wedged between a small wardrobe and the legs of a single seat table. Four weaved bags.

His heart pounded against the walls of his chest. His head began to swirl.

The sound of a siren broke him from the malaise. As he opened the front door, a paramedic jumped off of a motorcycle and retrieved a medical kit. He acknowledged Grayson as he hurried past and into the room.

The paramedic called a code into his radio and went to work with a series of checks before he pulled a defibrillator from his bag. He fired the paddles on to Niall's chest; the shock sent his body into a spasm. After the third attempt, two more paramedics rushed in to the room.

With resignation, they loaded Niall on to the stretcher and then into the back of an ambulance parked on the street front.

No sooner than loaded, the ambulance door shut, and the vehicle sped off, lights and sirens ablaze. The motorbike paramedic turned to Grayson.

'He'll be taken to Royal London, but it doesn't look good.'

The pandemonium subsided as the sirens faded. Onlookers retreated to their flats and went about their business. Grayson stood alone on the street.

The front gate now lay to the side of the concrete pathway, cast aside by the paramedics. As he entered the flat, the smell of sodden beer and body odour was apparent. He moved empty bottles off of the ledge and cleared the small table before opening the window.

On the table was an event flyer. An evening of boxing at *York Hall* on 6th January. At the top of the fight card read the names Grayson Day vs. Jake Ward, below the fighters described as 'the local prodigy' and the 'northern light'.

He dislodged the bags, brushed aside debris as he dragged them, two at a time, to the middle of the small room. As he pulled out the third and fourth bag, a pile of scrunched papers beneath the table drew his attention. He retrieved the three balls, unfolded them and placed them flat on the table.

Two were letters from Kamsi to Niall. The third was also handwritten, letters shaky, they struggled to stay on the lines. It finished abruptly.

Grayson first read the letters in Kamsi's handwriting. They revealed that Kamsi had collected several items that he had left in the *Cranbrook* flat when Niall was removed and she had kept them safely in her office in the *Community Centre*. She asked him to call her to arrange a time to meet. She wanted to return the items to him.

The second letter again asked to set up a time to meet. It also suggested that they could meet halfway between the *Cranbrook Estate* and the *Arden Estate*. The letter referenced an earlier conversation, where they agreed he needed to go into rehab. Then and only then, he could try to mend the relationship with Grayson. She promised that when he was in treatment, she would speak with Ama and Grayson and try to arrange for them to meet.

With reluctance, Grayson picked up the third piece of paper. It was unfinished, balled and thrown to the floor:

Ama

I'm sorry. She waited for me, but wouldn't give my things back. She pulled them, I pulled and she went into the road. There was nothing I could do. I could see the driver had called an ambulance, but when I heard the sirens, I panicked. Please tell Grayson I'm sorry. I'm sorry for everything, ever since Katlin I just don't kn...

The note finished abruptly.

Grayson pulled out items of clothing from the first two bags. Most of the pieces he recognised. They were his father's. Worn and faded, but they were his. Most noticeably a navy blue polo shirt with a white trim on the collar. It looked smaller than he remembered. It was the shirt his father had worn on their last adventure to *Guy's Hospital*, the day his mother had died. He remembered the cotton scratching his skin as his father pulled him tight. He couldn't breathe.

The third bag contained Grayson's old clothes and toys, Kamsi must have given them to Niall, after Grayson had outgrown or finished playing with them. His Thundercat t-shirt. A battleship game, mastermind and old packs of playing cards.

There was less in the final bag. What looked like

paperwork, Grayson removed two beige folders. The first held loose photos. He had seen them before. Some had been hung on the wall at their house on Old Ford Road. There was Niall and Katlin's wedding pictures. They looked so in love, so happy. A photo from their honeymoon in Cornwall. Grayson's baby photos and a mug shot of his first day at school. To his surprise, there were photos that Ama and Kamsi had taken. His twelfth birthday and a series from the Christmas dinners they hosted at the Community Centre. Ama and Kamsi's appearance unchanged, Grayson taller each year. The second folder contained pictures and press cuttings from Grayson's boxing career.

The final item he took from the bag was a drawing. A child's drawing of a house with a large tree in the garden. Next to the tree was a fire station and firemen by a red truck. By the house stood four figures, the last two hand-in-hand.

Grayson slumped to the chair, elbows to the table his head fell to his palms. He wept.

41 REPRESENT

28 JANUARY 2018

'Ams, are you ready?'

Ama emerged from her bedroom, apprehensive at the prospect of returning to Mass. Grayson questioned how she could maintain her faith in light of all the tragedy that she had undergone. Perhaps it was the reverse, and it was her faith that gave her the strength to keep going. Resplendent in an understated royal blue *Gele* and *Buba*, she took a deep breath, readied herself, gave him an affirmative nod and gentle hug as she passed through the door he held open. She was the strongest person he had ever known.

The elevator creaked as it slowed to a stop. As the doors opened, Grayson detected a scurry of voices fall to silence. Ama hadn't seemed to notice. He slowed, swinging his rucksack to his shoulder and letting Ama lead the way.

Pushing open the main door, she immediately stopped in her tracks.

Pastor Okereke was standing at the foot of the ramp, where just weeks before laid the tributes for Kamsi. A dozen church members flanked him. Friendly faces that Ama recognised. Beyond them was a large gathering of residents and neighbours. Each and everyone of them beaming bright at her. With a wide smile, the Pastor embraced Ama, still frozen in shock.

'Morning my dear,' he chuckled, offering Ama his hand, 'a small change of plans to this morning's service.'

Ama turned to Grayson, who gently laughed before encouraging her to accept the Pastor's hand and follow him. They walked a procession down the path, perhaps a hundred sets of eyes on them. At the gate of the Community Centre stood Namrata Nasrin, a friend and Bangladeshi resident who had assumed the role of Community Centre Manager. In an exchange, she took Ama's hand from the Pastor and continued the journey now inside the gate. The gathered crowd began to shuffle in anticipation, younger members with mobile phones in-hand taking pictures and capturing video.

Rather than guide them towards the Community Centre doors, the parting in the onlookers swung to the right, revealing a new installation. A decorative gate and waist high green fence that encompassed a previously inconspicuous and overgrown piece of land. The land was now soil, turned and cultivated ready to plant. A sign hung above the gate which read, 'Kamsi's Patch.'

Cranbrook Community Garden
Dedicated to the memory of Kamsi Olakunbi
Heart and soul forever with us, her spirit lives on

Grayson leaned forward offering Ama, one of her own handkerchiefs.

'Here, I thought you might need these.'

She pulled him close and squeezed. The embrace took him back to Guy's hospital. 'It's ok,' they both felt the unspoken words. As they parted, others moved in to hug Ama, passing on messages of love and hope in a small celebration of Kamsi's life. Grayson stepped back and watched on, Estella joined his side, her fingertips reached for his. As they touched, the two met with a smile.

Grayson would later explain to Ama that the garden would be landscaped and planted. That the residents would be able to enjoy a peaceful spot, amongst beautiful flowers, to relax and reflect. They could also join with other members of the Community to grow vegetables, make homemade produce and crafts.

No doubt she would question how the community could pay for such a beautiful dedication. He would tell her that the residents had had a whip round and just before the deadline an anonymous donor gave thirty thousand pounds to ensure the completion of the project and its maintenance for many years to come.

The garden would not bring Kamsi back, but it would give the Community a space to remember her and a route towards healing.

Three figures approached on the path. He was expecting them and made his way across to meet them outside of the gate. Before any of them could speak, Grayson swung the bag off his shoulder and passed it to the more senior man.

'It's all in there. Plus a little extra for your trouble,' his look had a stern sincerity.

Turning his head to guide their attention to the large crowd of neighbours and friends.

'Sorry. Our deal is off. There will be no sale here. We'll be fighting this one.'

♠ End ♠